Border Run

A NOVEL

Simon Lewis

Sort Of
BOOKS

Also by Simon Lewis

Bad Traffic

Go

www.simonlewiswriter.com

Border Run

A NOVEL

Simon Lewis

THANKS

For their help and support: Mark and Nat, Rough Guides, Anna deVries, Nikky Twyman, Mark South, David Leffman, Du, Xiaoshan, Xiaosong, Yen, Fraze and Liz, Ed and Fran, Gags, Charlie, Mark Pengelly, Angela, Shen Ye, Daren, Howard, Qian Fan, Dan Brown, Elaine, Sveta, Charles, Darren, Will, Nicola, Annie, Vero and Alex, Mum and Dad of course, the Royal Society of Authors, and all in Kunming, Ruili and Dali. Thanks.

Sort Of Books, PO Box 18678, London NW3 2FL

Typeset in Melior and Frutiger to a design by Henry Iles

Printed in the UK by Clays Ltd, St Ives PLC
on Forest Stewardship Council (mixed sources) certified paper

Distributed by Profile Books
3a Exmouth House, Pine Street, London EC1R OJH

in all territories excluding the United States and Canada

Typeset in Melior Medium to a design by Henry Iles

224pp

A catalogue record for this book is available
from the British Library

ISBN 978-0956308658

For Noe and Hana

Border Run

1

"Listen. Wake up. I've sorted us out a little adventure. An adventurette. Just for one day. We're going on a trip." Jake opened the curtains. "You're always on about how you should be getting up early 'cause that's when the light is best. And you are right. It is beautiful. None of that glare you get later on that causes the harsh shadows. Lovely."

Will rose to his elbows and, with sleepy befuddlement, put names to shapes: wardrobe, rucksack, TV, chair. A thermos the size of an aqua-lung, stoppered with a cork. A print of two boggle-eyed fish. Brown stains on the ceiling like a map of an archipelago. Chunky dials on the face of a bedside cabinet, none of which seemed to do anything. He could not recall the name of this hotel or the town they were in. He had the sense of a vast and forbidding foreignness beyond the door that he was not yet ready to face. He rubbed his eyes. "What are you on about?"

"I've been up for an hour already, and I've sorted us out this amazing opportunity. We're going to a secret waterfall. You'll want to pack a bag. Shorts, T-shirt, swimming trunks. The guy's waiting outside."

"What guy?"

"Howard's this laid-back type, only slightly weird. He lives here, and he knows all these amazing secret places in the forest, and he's going to take us to one. For free. It's a rare opportunity which will not even cost us any money, and we do not want to miss it."

"Where did you meet him?"

"I was having breakfast at that noodle place, and he found me. He knows everything about this place, even speaks the lingo. He told me about this amazingly beautiful spot that only the tribals know about, it isn't in any guidebooks or anything. It's so lovely—"

"How do you know?"

"I've had it evoked for me; the man has a striking turn of phrase. We chill out, we go swimming, we have a picnic, you take pictures, the sun shines, the water is warm, the birds sing, the tribal people are colourful and interesting. I didn't tell you about the tribal people. The photogenic Wa people, living in harmony with nature. Throw some stuff in a bag."

"I don't want to be forced into doing something I haven't agreed to."

"But I already told him that you'd come."

"That was a bit . . . presuming, then, wasn't it? I haven't even had any breakfast. I thought we were going to go and look at the tea factory."

"A tea factory? Come on, really?"

"Then get the bus to the Laos border."

"Just 'cause you haven't written it in your day planner doesn't mean we can't do it. What does it matter when we get to Laos?"

"I don't understand. Yesterday you said you couldn't wait to get there. You said—"

"I'm seeing fascinating sets of photos of tribal people and jungle. I'm thinking that will be two very impressive albums displaying an adventurous spirit." Jake folded his arms. "Anyway, I'm going. Up to you whether you want to come along."

"That's not fair, is it? I'd have to wait for you to get back."

"You get the bus to Laos, and I'll meet you there."

"What, really? But . . . I thought . . . we're supposed to be travelling together." Aware that a plaintive tone had entered his voice, Will consciously lowered it for the next statement: "We do stuff together and make joint decisions."

"You can make the next decision. Anything you want: any temple, museum, or archaeological site that proves to be a hole in the ground, wherever you want to go to, we go there."

"I really don't understand why you're so hot all of a sudden to take a drive into the countryside. Like you've never seen a waterfall."

"It's good not to just do what everyone else does, to get off the mango smoothie trail for once and discover a bit of real life. You said that. I'm just saying back at you what you said to me. He's down there waiting for us."

Will got out of bed and looked out the window. A Jeep was parked in the road outside the guesthouse and a scrawny white man wearing a red bandana leaned against it, smoking.

"What does he do?"

"What do you mean?"

"You said he lives here. He must have a job or something."

"I don't know. He mentioned starting up a tour agency."

"How can we trust him?"

"What's he going to do, sell us into slavery?"

"He looks like a bum."

"Sure. I imagine he has an alcohol problem, a notebook full of poetry, and a lot of little bags."

"If you've got him nailed, why are you so keen to hang out with him?"

"He knows the score round here, and we don't. Come on, you're the one always banging on about we should do something a bit different and have a proper adventure, here's a chance. It's just one day. Come on. For the fans."

"I wish I'd brought a tripod. Waterfalls need long exposures."

Jake slapped his shoulder. "Good man."

2

Howard was lithe and heavily tanned, with a wrinkled neck and veiny, big-knuckled hands. A bandana swept long stringy hair back from his forehead; Will supposed it hid a receding hairline. Howard unrolled a map across the bonnet of his Jeep, laying it flat with Will's camera on one corner, his bag on another. It was labelled in Chinese and showed the province, Yunnan, down in the far southwest of the country. Howard laid his finger on a dot in the bottom corner. "We're here. Right near the border with Burma." Here, the red dots that marked towns were far apart, with just a few narrow lines connecting them.

The finger was nicotine-stained, with a big whorled knuckle, and it bore a silver ring of a skull with a snake's head coming out of the eye socket, the snake's body forming the band. It headed south and west, following a yellow line, then veered off and entered the map's emptiest quarter, a smudge of undifferentiated green. "All this here is hills and jungle. There're just a few villages and trails. Now they're smashing tracks into it. In ten years' time they'll have chopped down the trees for rubber plantations and the tribals will be waiting tables, but for now it's good and wild. There's a new track right here. And it's pretty dry at the moment, so I reckon I can get the beast" – he slapped the Jeep – "down there. All the way to the end of the road, which is about here." His finger tapped.

Will frowned. "It looks quite a long way."

"It's early, we'll have lots of time there. It's beautiful. Old-growth forest and a waterfall. It's all free, I'm paying for petrol. Put the bags in the back, the trunk lid is jammed."

"What about breakfast?" said Will.

"I got some steamed buns. And your friend here got us a picnic for later. So we're all set."

Howard drove past shuttered shops. At a noodle stall, men bent like scholars over bowls. A scooter passed with a couple of chickens trussed up on the back, another with buckets of white rubber. Then they passed a string of garages on the outskirts of town, where one man squatted welding, holding a dark oblong glass before the torch. The guidebook called this town an interesting stop off the highway to Laos, offering the opportunity to sample produce at the Thousand Treasures tea factory and visit an interesting nineteenth-century *wat* on the outskirts of town. Will found it hard to imagine a foreigner living here – what could be done all day?

Howard asked, "How long have you spent in country?"

"We flew into Hong Kong," said Will, "and we've been working our way west for three weeks now, going to all the usual places. Yangshuo, Lijiang, all that. Laos next, then Thailand, then home." Surely Jake had covered this already? "So this trip, I wasn't sure I liked it when you said—"

Howard turned off the tarmac road onto a track, and immediately a noisy rumble filled the Jeep, making conversation impossible. What on the map had been a confident yellow line turned out to a winding red mud track peppered with potholes. Bushes and bamboo groves offered glimpses of rice and tea fields beyond. Will dozed off and awoke to see a man in uniform waving them down. More guys squatted around a plastic sheet, playing cards. Muddy motorbikes leaned against trees.

Howard stopped the Jeep, saying, "It's a customs patrol."

"Why?" asked Will.

"Burma's just over there." Howard pointed at the dense wall of foliage. "That's a fucked-up place, and this is a long, lonely border. A lot of naughtiness goes back and forth."

"Like what?"

"Teak, jade, drugs. Refugees."

"They'll search the Jeep?"

"They're not interested in us. We're just tourists on a tour. Civilians."

"How is Burma fucked up?"

"It's all warlords fighting over the opium crop. One of these armies is led by a ten-year-old kid, seriously. He has visions, and his followers do whatever crazy shit he comes up with."

Will leaned forward, frowning. "Really? Round here? Are we close?"

"It's not far. But relax, kid. This is the right side of the border. Nothing happening here. You're safe with Uncle Howard."

The official picked his way around a pothole. Howard lit a cigarette and blew smoke out the window. "There's no sure thing here. I don't want to get anyone's hopes up."

"What do you mean?"

Howard motioned at Jake, who was asleep, then said, "He didn't mention it?"

"Mention what?"

"He didn't say anything about the girls?"

"No," said Will.

"I thought he would have mentioned that when he told you about the trip."

"What girls?"

"I went down once before. This honey was swimming. I gave her space, I didn't want to intrude – I mean, she was enjoying a private moment. But she waved me over. She came out of the water and walked up to me like it was the first day on a new planet and we were the only people on it. No self-consciousness at all. And very naked. And she was hot. Only not like she knew she was hot – there was no 'look at me naked here, all dripping wet' about it. She just smiled and – well, I don't want to go into the details of the beautiful thing that proceeded to happen. I'm just saying it was game on, couldn't resist if I wanted to. And you can see I'm no looker. Just a very natural thing taking place there on the forest floor, on the carpet of leaves."

"Oh."

"See, what it is, the Wa girls out there in the forest got this thing in their culture called 'walking marriage'. Means if a Wa girl takes a fancy to you, she can pull you away to a cosy corner for some fun and no one's going to think anything of it. It's not like there's going to be any comeback afterwards. It's like, for them, they're fulfilling another bodily function. A need being simply . . . indulged."

"I see."

"Tribal girls, the ones deep in the forest, they haven't got hang-ups like the brittle city bitches you always meet. It's something about living close to nature. No politics there, no power games. They don't care that you can't speak to them. Seriously, it doesn't bother them at all. 'Cause there's a whole other language, the language of men and women, no vocal cords required. Just consensual adults enjoying each other's bodies, like nature intended."

"And this is what you said to Jake?"

He drummed his hands on the steering wheel. "There's no promises being made or anything. Probably we won't see anyone, and honestly, it wouldn't matter if we didn't, 'cause it's a special place."

"I'm sure."

The official wore green fatigues with epaulettes, but what seemed to mark his status was the neat short hair, glistening with product, and his white gloves. The gloves were intriguing: impossible not to see them without wondering how he kept them so pristine. When the man looked through the windscreen, his blankly professional mask slipped, and his eyes widened in surprise. Presumably he didn't see many whities, and here were three all together: the scrawny middle-aged guide in the bandana, driving, and his two sleepy young charges in the back, still fresh-faced despite the tan and stubble.

The official peered closer and opened his mouth and looked tentative, the white fingers fluttering like he was working his way up to say something. A card player

barked, and he called back. Howard muttered, "He's saying we're Westerners. He's going to wave us on. Come
on, little man, wave us on." The official frowned his way
back into character, and the hand regained its certainty. It
twisted sharply, and the fingers bent: come forward. The
men were dismissed. "See?" said Howard. "Civilians."

He waved at the card players as he passed. "That's
right, guys, don't trouble yourselves on our behalf. Will
you look at this trail? Be gone in a few months; soon as
it rains, it'll be washed away. We'll be there in no time."

Now the track was a twisting strip of red earth ripped
through a dim green hall. Trees craned over it, cutting
out much of the light, and it seemed to Will like they
were lurking, impatient to repair this ugly red scar.
Apart from a few short steep downhills ending in brack-
ish puddles, they were heading upwards. Howard ran
the engine hard, never quite getting enough acceleration
to move out of first gear. Clearly no other four-wheeled
vehicle had attempted the journey recently, and since
turning on to the trail they hadn't seen anyone besides
the cops.

Howard stopped the Jeep. He pointed at roofs, visible
above the line of the trees, a hundred metres or so up the
slope from the track. "I got to announce our presence at
the village. Only polite. You got to approach them the
right way. Remember, this track is new; until last year it
would have taken days to walk from here to anywhere
civilised, so they're still not used to visitors. I'll be back
in a couple of minutes. You see anyone, smile, nod, don't
make any threatening gestures."

"We can't come with you?"

"Five minutes." Howard headed up a trail and in moments was gone.

Will got out of the Jeep. He took pictures, aiming downhill at lush hills fading into mist, dew-dappled greenery. These would be attractive images, yet unsatisfactory: they would not capture what he felt, which was a peculiar sense, a cousin to vertigo, of being farther out than he ever had before.

He clicked through the images on the camera display: fruit stall, man selling eggs boiled in tea, banana and rubber plantations. It was a pity that most of the people were in the middle ground, or had their backs turned, but he felt too awkward sticking his camera in people's faces. One film was stored on the SD card, dated from two months ago. He played it through, as he did at idle moments every day, and always with the same shame-faced sense of giving in to a dubious, illicit pleasure: twenty seconds of wobbly footage of maybe-or-maybe-not girlfriend Jess, sitting cross-legged in a tent in shorts, ticking off the bands she would like to see on her fingers. Every time he watched it, he found himself drawn to something different, and this time it was to the movement of the blue-painted fingernails. He imagined telling her about this – "So on the spur of the moment we went on this ride with a hippie right into the forest, to places that aren't in any guidebooks." She would be impressed, and that made him feel better about it, it gave the trip a sense of purpose. "'Cause it's important sometimes to get off the trail. Rather than living in a mango-smoothie bubble, just going where everyone else goes." Of course, it would be nothing without some good photos.

Jake cuffed his shoulder. "Caught you. I can't believe you're watching that again. Listen to this." He was reading out of the guidebook. "It's got a bit about Wa people in here. Says they used to be headhunters." He tapped Will on the shoulder. "It says here travellers have been disappearing in the area."

"What? Really?"

"Yeah. Maybe they're still taking heads. In secret. No one knows we're here, do they? We could just . . . vanish."

"It'll be fine," said Will uneasily. "Howard seems to know his way around."

"What if it's a trap? What if they're paying the hippie to bring Westerners right to them? Then . . . shlork." Jake drew a finger across his neck.

"Don't be stupid."

"I'm just saying. Look at the way he ran off just now. What's that about? How do we know there aren't a bunch of guys creeping up on us as we speak? Have you got a weapon? Just in case we have to defend ourselves."

"I've got my Swiss army knife."

"We'd be better off running. I don't know, though. I'm guessing these people would be pretty good trackers. Imagine that – being hunted through the forest. Running, panicking . . . You could run, you could hide, but I reckon they'd get you in the end."

"Show me what it says."

"One or two every year just gone. There's a warning. And a skull and crossbones."

"I knew it was a bad idea," snapped Will. "I shouldn't have let you talk me into it. And all 'cause you think there's an off chance of getting some action. It's starting to annoy me, the way you run around with your tongue hanging out all the time." A sly look in Jake's eyes brought him short. "What exactly does it say? Show me. Give it here. Give me the book."

Jake held it away from him. "Says they especially go for freckly photographer types. They shrink the heads and use them as ashtrays. They make puppets out of the hands."

"Oh, ha ha," said Will, annoyed at himself for not seeing the windup.

Jake said, "What do you mean about my tongue?"

"He told me about walking marriage."

"And obviously that's all I'm interested in."

"We are supposed to be doing things that people do when they are on holiday, which is . . . not just leching. What's going on? I should still be in bed. I should be having a mango smoothie. I just . . . Where are we? With who?"

"The irony, of course, is that it's you that needs to get laid," Jake pointed out.

"I've got a girlfriend."

"Well . . . you haven't really, though, have you?"

"What do you mean by that?"

With a rustle of leaves, Howard slid down the slope and joined them. "Are we good?"

"Great," said Jake.

They drove on through dense forest. Leafy branches batted the windscreen. In places, landslides had carried the track away. Howard would ease the Jeep across the muddy slope, muttering, "Come on, beasty, there we go," while Will braced and tried not to look down. This trip was taking much longer than he had thought, and it seemed like a lot of hassle, a lot of petrol to be burning, for the nebulous goal of his own enjoyment. Contrary to expectation, it seemed unlikely that there could be much to shoot around here; the eye got lost in a hopeless mass of tedious green detail.

The only evidence of civilisation was the track, and that was empty. The last people they had seen were the cops, a long way behind. Will felt anxious, then disappointed in himself for feeling that. Jake wasn't worried, so why should he be? Anyway, he told himself, he was with friends, and anything that might happen, any crash or breakdown, could be dealt with. He allayed his fears by imagining himself narrating the story, in a quiet pub or student union bar, to Jess: "Bit of a prang, driver injured, we had to walk through the forest for hours to get help, leeches were a bitch, found some tribals, they made a splint out of bark . . ."

Howard braked and turned off the engine. The track had petered out. The rattling Will had received seemed to carry on, repeating like an echo, as he got out and stretched. Howard led them forward, and Will realised belatedly that there was a lot of noise going on – a buzz had risen imperceptibly and now seemed all around. They came out from under the green canopy into sudden light and space. A steep-sided canyon yawned at their feet. Roaring white plumes of water fell twenty metres or so over glossy rock into a pool that was marvellously still and blue in comparison. It was fringed by a little beach and an elegant frill of forest green. Beyond the pool, the river frothed as it kinked between boulders along the canyon floor.

"See?" said Howard with pride, as if the spectacle had been produced in response to a challenge. "There you are. A secret waterfall."

"This is really nice," said Will. He was wishing he had a tripod. With a slow shutter speed, the cascade of water would show up as silky white strips. Shame, too, that he hadn't got a circular polariser to increase colour saturation and cut out glare. Still, a large aperture and narrow depth of field would create intriguing effects. That rainbow hovering over the base of the torrent would come out well with a low ISO and a longish exposure. He realised that a pale oval on the surface of the water was not a rock, lowered the camera, and pointed. "There's someone down there."

"Oh," said Jake. "Naked ladies. Wow."

3

A girl was swimming in the pool. Long black hair fanned out over the water, anchoring the shimmering image of her body below. She saw the foreigners and pointed them out to a second girl, treading water. Both girls swam to the side of the pool, climbed onto a boulder and squatted, looking up, shading their eyes with their hands. They wore only black knickers and were young and slim and dripping wet. Will stood dumbly still, feeling like a busted voyeur. "Well, this is awkward," he said.

"They'll be cool," said Howard. "Relax. Go down and say hello. And it's like I said, you never know."

Jake contemplated the pool. "You could just about jump in from here. That would be some entrance."

"I wouldn't recommend it," said Howard. "You don't know how deep it is. The path is there. See? Be careful, it's steep."

"You're not coming?"

"I want to have a look at the engine; she's making this pinking noise. Go on."

The cliff face was almost vertical, and the narrow path, barely discernible in places, zigzagged between rocks and exposed roots.

Jake, in the lead, stepping sure-footed, said, "Could you believe this ride? I feel like the snowman in a snow globe. One that's full of nails, not snow. You know my theory? There is no tour agency." The path banked sharply around a rock. Jake swung himself acrobatically around it on a trailing root.

Will shimmied down on hands and knees. Whenever he glimpsed the rocks below he gnawed his lip, closed his eyes and counted to five. He wanted to keep his gaze firmly locked on the ground and on his feet, but he had to keep looking up to bat thorns out of the way or find roots to cling to. "Why, why, why do you think that?"

"He's lonely, needs some of his own tribe to talk to. Shit, I nearly fell over. You get near the bottom, you think you're there, and you stop concentrating, and bosh, broken ankle. You know what I reckon? He's on the run. I bet he killed his wife back home and he's been lying low ever since."

The path levelled out. Will's knees had help during the descent, but now they were shaky. He put a hand on Jake's shoulder. They considered the girls, who seemed as skittish and beautiful as deer. Will was sure that at any moment they would unfreeze, turn and run.

"Wish I'd learned some Chinese," said Jake. "If I'd known this was going to happen, I definitely would have." He called out, "We're sorry to disturb you. Do you mind? We wanted to go swimming. Do you speak English? No?"

"Hello," called one girl, and put a hand over her mouth to cover her giggles.

"I love you," called the second. They whispered to each other, heads together, then each tried out the other's phrase, adding it to her own: "Hello, I love you," "I love you, hello." Having got the hang of the words, they began to chant, "Hello, I love you, I love you, hello," which caused much amusement.

Jake took off his T-shirt. The girls stared at his torso, impressed with his muscular physique, perhaps, or fascinated by its subtle unfamiliarity. He ran splashing hard into the water and launched himself forward. The girls clapped and shouted encouragement. Treading water, he called back at Will, "We have to give the impression of being fun, sexy guys. Let's splash each other. Try not to stare at their tits; that'll creep them out."

Will put his camera in his bag, tucked it behind a rock, decided it was precarious there and put it behind a different rock, then took off his T-shirt and waded tensely in, bracing against the cold. He breaststroked to Jake with his head held high.

"Remember," said Jake. "Cocky and funny equals laid."

"How can I be funny? They don't even speak English."

"Let's splash each other."

Jake and Will circled, splashing. The stratagem worked: the girls came off the rock into the water and began to circle and splash each other, too, then, quite quickly and naturally, as if there were no intention behind it, they came closer until the ripples of activity intersected. Jake splashed a girl, then they were all splashing together, and the tinkle of girlish laughter rose above the background buzz of the falls.

Will found himself targeting and being targeted by the smaller of the girls. He wondered how that decision had been made and who had made it. She darted forward and stroked his arm like a kid at the zoo daring to reach through the bars. He was pulled underneath and came up spluttering. Jake, the culprit, grinned and swam away. Will lunged at him, and the guys play-fought. Again Will felt himself dragged under. This time it was his girl. His ankle seemed to tingle where she had gripped it.

Will looked at her, rainbow, beach, waterfall, and thought that here were all the components required for happiness, though he was too self-conscious to really feel it. She dived again and came up alongside him, and her foot slid slowly and deliberately – unequivocally, undeniably – up his leg. She grinned.

4

Will guessed she was in her late teens, but it was hard to tell, she could have been anywhere from seventeen to thirty. Her very dark eyes were far apart, and there wasn't much bridge to her nose. It made her face intriguingly alien in aspect – also, almost unbearably cute.

She had a broad mouth, and when she smiled, she looked young and mischievous. Her lips at rest protruded in a sultry pout. Judging by the way she often covered her mouth with her hand, she clearly thought that her worst feature. He wanted to find a way to tell her to be proud of it, it was adorable.

She beckoned for him to follow and ploughed off towards the waterfall. He swam behind in a kind of dream until spray was prickling his face. Currents churned the water, and all he could hear was the torrent's buzz. The girl dived, and he was quick to believe that she was lost to him, as he couldn't help the suspicion that he didn't deserve such easy familiarity and approval. But he saw her again behind the wall of water, waving with her head cocked, grinning with delight at sharing her secret: a hidden cave. He went down and forward, water drummed on his scalp, then he came up alongside her.

Dripping rock sloped back, as if some giant mouth had taken a bite out of the rock face. The misty space was just big enough for the two of them to stand upright. Half a watermelon was wedged at the back, presumably put there to keep cool. She took a knife out of it and cut two slices.

Looking back through the screen of water, Will saw Jake and the other girl stepping hand in hand across rocks at the far side of the pool. They stopped and kissed. He could see well despite the distortions of the water, but supposed they couldn't see him at all. They broke apart and carried on out of sight behind a boulder.

"Wow, this is great. Really great." Will smiled and nodded, reflected that he'd been doing that a lot, and worried he was starting to look dumb and insincere. They were standing very close. She dropped her watermelon rind, wiped her mouth, then spread her slim fingers on the base of her throat and said, "Qiong Mei." Her wet hair was a slick black comma curling round her neck and pointing at her breasts, which she seemed no more bothered by or self-conscious about than her elbows. Will was bothered about them, though, aware of them hovering at the edge of the shot as he looked at her face.

He pointed at her. "Qiong Mei." It seems he was saying it wrong, and she really wanted him to say it right, so he persevered until she was satisfied. He got it right, it seemed, only when he blurted it in a tone of exasperation. He put a finger on his chest and said, "Will."

"While," she said, the effort making her frown. She tried it again as a kind of little hiccup – "Wheel" – and her brows rose as if in surprise, her eyes widening. They giggled together. Mentally, Will congratulated himself – it seemed to be going so well; better, in fact, than most of his encounters with girls who did speak English. But there was anxiety alongside the triumph: the novelty of parroting each other's names would soon fade; how could this level of fun and intimacy be sustained?

"Yes, very good."

"Wheel."

"Chong May."

"Whale."

Okay, now what? "Shong Mai."

She stood on her toes and put her hand flat on top of her head. When she moved it across, they discovered that even on tiptoe she barely came up to his sternum, and this seemed a point of considerable interest to her. Will supposed he must look huge to her. She seemed possessed with a scientific urge to categorise how much bigger he was, and searched out other startling comparisons. They found out that his thumb and forefingers could almost encircle her arm, and that when their palms were pressed together the tips of her fingers didn't reach even his second knuckle.

Privately, Will was making another set of notes, on qualities of smoothness and shininess, the diverting landscape of dips and curves. Her limbs were lithe and toned, her skin smooth and flawless. Work-worn stubby fingers and chafed heels seemed her only imperfections. He kept noticing all over again how beautiful she was.

She moved closer, sliding an arm around him and resting a hand lightly on his lower back. The hand doodled up and down. Her nipple seemed to sizzle against his side. He felt dumb and lucky, fizzling with expectation. Astonishingly, it seemed that this was really going to happen, and it seemed certain to be one of the highlights of his life thus far. Aware that he was shaking a little, he told himself to relax and be more like Jake, carefree, easy in his body, going with the flow. As her hip pressed against his, he felt a lump in his pocket.

5

"Oh shit, my wallet." He took it out. "How daft is that? I went swimming with my wallet. It's all wet now."

The leather was slippery, and Will's fingers were damp; he dropped it as soon as he got it out. Notes splayed out and flopped over the rock. Will and the girl stooped to gather the currency, shuffling, careful not to lose their footing, and he prattled, "How daft is that, sorry, sorry. I've got so much of this little stuff, I should have changed it all up."

She handed him a passport photograph. "Oh," he said. It was his lucky picture. Jessica's face loomed in the foreground, her foreshadowed chin at the bottom of frame. Will and Jake bent together behind, their heads touching. All three were pulling faces. The photo had been taken in a train station photo booth. He and Jake had been on their way to Heathrow, and she had been there to say goodbye. They'd had such a laugh, crammed together in there, that a guard had come to see what was going on. Her smile seemed to expand out of the picture, and her big, upraised eyes were looking right at him.

Will gnawed his lip. "That's my girlfriend. Well. Kind of. I don't know. It's complicated." He tucked the photo away and put the wallet back in his pocket. But he still felt her presence. "She's called Jessica. I'm not even sure she is my girlfriend. She said she was worried that our relationship was in a bit of a rut. So we're on a sort of trial separation. To be honest, it's all a bit up in the air. We email each other a lot. Well, I write to her, mostly."

The girl started to stroke the back of his neck. Will said, "I want to give it another shot with her." She went to kiss him, and he pushed her away. "The thing is . . . I'm not a very good liar. When I go back and she asks me, 'Did you cop off with anyone?' I would . . . She would know. She just would. She knows me so well. And the door that is a little bit open for me at the moment would, I think, definitely close. So, I mean, don't get me wrong, I really like you, I mean you're fantastic, really very attractive. Probably the most attractive person who's ever shown any interest in me, but . . . I'm going to have to regretfully decline."

Will stepped away, feeling dumb and gauche. The girl cooed an attempt at his name, and he turned to see her with a hand on her hip, pouting over her shoulder, chin lowered and eyes raised, lashes fluttering. It made her seem worldly and knowing, which made him feel more awkward.

He took another step back, and she grabbed his hand. "Hey, no, really. I'm sorry." He pulled his hand away, slipped, fell, and slid into the torrent of water, which drummed on his head. Thrashing, Will banged both elbows and a knee, then was tumbling in cold darkness. He struck out, bashed an elbow again, and came up spluttering on the other side of the falls.

Sore and smarting, he headed for the beach. He took out his emergency kit and, wincing, applied antibacterial lotion to his grazes. He had thrown away a sure thing, and he did not even have the warm glow of righteousness as a reward, because he knew that it was only the appearance of the photograph that had stopped him from straying. He was glad he couldn't see Jake, aware that his friend would look poorly on him for this. It was galling to have done the right thing for no reward.

The girl was swimming slowly towards him. He didn't want to try and talk to her, and he was sure that she was coming after him out of pity or a sense of social obligation. Maybe she would assume he was gay.

He decided to head back up the cliff. The best shots would be from the canyon rim; he had not explored all the options earlier. He could come down slowly, shooting all the way. He told himself that he had a job to do, and the success of this expedition would be measured on the quality of the images.

The girl called his name again. She was heading up, too. She was certainly persistent. Perhaps she wouldn't mind being in a few pictures, though he'd have to get her to put some clothes on, certainly if he wanted to post them on Facebook or show them to Jess.

When Will got to the top, he saw Howard leaning against the Jeep, smoking. He was about to call a greeting when he realised his guide was not alone. Two men were approaching. They were bare-chested and wore green combat trousers and plimsolls and had knife sheaths hanging from rope belts. They carried between them a bulging hessian sack. Might there be some problem?

Perhaps they were bandits who would love to get their hands on a fancy camera. It was unlikely, but you never knew. Deciding it wise not to make himself known yet, Will crouched in the long grass to watch.

6

One man greeted Howard with a raised hand. The second spat a forceful stream of red chewing betel, which spattered against the wheel of the Jeep, then he grinned, and Will saw how he managed the trick: one front tooth was missing.

It was not a robbery, only a couple of local guys come round to chat. Perhaps they would agree to be photographed. Will rose to his feet and took a step, but when he saw Howard open the boot, he came to a stuttering halt. Howard had told him that the boot was broken. Something was amiss here. He sank once more into the grass, glad to have remained unnoticed.

The men laid the sack in the boot. Howard closed the lid, locked it, then leaned on it to check it was secure. He offered a packet of cigarettes; each man took two, lighting one and tucking the second behind an ear. Then they turned and stepped away and were swallowed by the green in an instant. It was over. The whole encounter had taken barely twenty seconds.

Now Howard was making an odd scraping motion with his foot. It was only when Will thought how doglike the gesture was that he realised what the old hippie was up to – kicking fresh dirt over the betel stain to conceal it. That meant he didn't want it seen. Will's suspicions were confirmed: something illicit was happening. Presumably, there was nothing wrong with the engine, and Howard had remained up here to meet the men and pick up the cargo.

"Wi-ee?" The girl was calling. She was coming up the path. She shouted again, louder. "Wi-ee?" Will couldn't think of anything to do to shut her up.

Howard frowned, came forward, and saw him. "Hey," he said lightly, "what you doing down there?"

Will felt sheepish and, as he rose, reminded himself that he was the injured party here, with a right to an indignation that he did not yet feel. "Who were they?"

"Oh, just some guys. They wanted to have a look at the Jeep. They'd never seen such a fine-looking vehicle before. All they've ever seen are those little three-wheel tractors."

It was not the reaction he'd expected, and it was disarming, but Howard seemed a little too friendly, too casual. Will let a silence stretch to see if he would carry on explaining. Howard shifted his weight from one leg to the other.

"They put something in the Jeep," said Will.

"They certainly did. Homegrown vegetables. It's all organic round here."

"I'd like to have a look. In the boot."

"The what?"

"The boot."

"I'm not wearing boots. But if I was, you could look in them."

37

"I guess you would call it the trunk."

"Oh, you say 'boot' for 'trunk,' huh? Is that an all-over-England thing, or just your particular dialect?"

"I want to have a look in the trunk."

"You never seen a vegetable before?"

"Would you unlock the trunk for me to have a look in it?"

"You'll just get your hands dirty. I hear a pretty girl calling your name. Seems like you made a friend. Why don't you go say hello?"

"You being weird and defensive just makes me suspicious."

"I'm not being weird and defensive. I'm lightening the mood. 'Cause you're bringing some negative vibes down on a beautiful experience."

"It looks like smuggling to me."

"It does? That's what it looks like?"

"Burma is just over there, right? I guess the other side of this river. And there's a lot going on in Burma, isn't there, as you've mentioned? Opium growing, for example. We're really out in the sticks here. A long way from any border patrols. Be easy to bring something over."

"You like to make these . . . suppositions. You have a talent for it."

"Only it would be difficult to get these illegal goods farther up into China, wouldn't it, what with all the checkpoints on the roads, the border patrols. But an odd thing about these checkpoints, like you said yourself, like we saw on the way here, is they don't search Jeeps with foreigners in. 'Cause that's tourists on a tour. Civilians. So let's say someone did want to get some dodgy goods up into China. What better way than to con a couple of travellers, get them to ride with you down to the border? Spin them some shit about starting up a tour agency, needing—"

Howard stepped forward and began speaking rapidly over him. "Now you're freaking me out with your rampant paranoia. You're not thinking straight. The sun has got to you, and I suggest a lie-down."

Will said, "I'm going to have a look in the boot."

Howard grabbed his arm. "Let's not do anything rash here."

"There'll be a customs check on the way back. Maybe I'll have a chat with those guys when we get there."

Howard squeezed. "You had an experience you can remember for the rest of your days. Why ruin it?"

"Stop it, you're hurting. How is that going to help?"

Howard let go and raised his hands, palms up. "Sorry. We're just talking. Tell them for what? You'll get us all arrested. Why not leave it be? Practise acceptance, like a Buddhist."

"I don't see why I should leave it be."

Grass swished behind him and, suspecting the smugglers' return, Will spun round. But it was the girl arriving, dusty and out of breath. She took in the scene, smiling uncertainly, and stood with one knee bent, an arm across her breasts. Obviously, she could sense the tension: her eyes darted back and forth as she tried to read tone and expressions. Howard pointed at her. "One word about this to anyone, and those two pretty little girls are going to be in a heap of shit."

"What have they got to do with anything?"

"That one was yours, right? If you shoot your mouth off, there will be serious consequences for that girl. She won't have done her job properly."

"Her job?"

"To keep you out of the way. If you haven't been kept out of the way, which you clearly haven't, and then you end up fucking this thing up, then it's going to be her fault, isn't it? And some scary people, whom you fortunately haven't met and you really don't want to meet, these scary people going to take it out on her, that's what I'm saying. And her friend, too, I'd guess. I'm a pussycat, I'm soft as a sack of shit, which is I believe another charming Britishism. But these people, the people I work for, they are quite nasty. Really scary fuckers. I'm scared of them. And I don't scare easy."

It occurred to Will to hit Howard. A hard, mean idea, it shocked him to even think it. He had never attacked anyone before. He even sought out his target – there, below the cheek, above the angle of the jaw. He would get his shoulder into it, and the impact would jar his arm. The man's head would snap back, and damage would have been done – but, better than that, the old hippie's certainty and self-control would fall away. Will wanted to see the man as reduced and anxious as he felt.

"I'm sorry. Really." Howard rubbed his stubble, then laid a hand on Will's shoulder. He was brotherly, apologetic, as he said, "No one can protect those girls. They're Burmese refugees, and their lives are cheap. Fucking guys for money is all they've ever known. And they're owned by nasty individuals who would kill them as soon as blink. So this, what you think you've seen here, it goes no further. Not now, not ever." He pointed. "For her sake."

Will stepped back, and the hand slipped off. "How do you live with yourself?"

"This is the easiest job they've ever had, and they're getting more for it than they'd normally make in six months. If it weren't for me, they'd be at the highway, fucking truckers for a bowl of rice." Howard put an arm around the girl, and she snuggled into his shoulder. But her smile didn't reach the upraised eyes, which nervously scanned his face. "This, for them, it's Christmas. Now that you understand the situation, I'm hoping we've got a deal."

"They really don't search Jeeps with foreigners? Not at all?"

"A couple of years back, Japanese tourists got searched; they couldn't see what it was about, made a complaint, called it harassment. And over stuff like this, the people here are very sensitive. They want you to have a good time in their country. Word came down, leave the foreigners alone. If it makes you feel more secure, I've done this four, five times. Find a couple of horny backpackers, take them on a tour, arrange for them to have a good time, transport a little merchandise. Everyone's happy, and there's never been the slightest issue. So you can relax."

Will went to the edge of the cliff. Far below he could see Jake and his girl entwined on a flat boulder. It looked a romantic spot, with the sun coming through the treetops to dapple the rock with sunlight, and the rapids frothing around them.

Howard said, "Have we got a deal?"

"It's not a deal, is it? It's a threat. It's blackmail."

41

"Hey, man." Howard sounded genuinely hurt. "That is a very harsh interpretation of events. I have only outlined the eventualities that will occur if you continue stubbornly to head down the path that you seem to be headed. I am being peace-and-love here, I just don't want anyone to get hurt. Have we got an understanding?"

"I won't say anything to Jake about your little racket."

"Not now and not later, either. Not ever. 'Cause these consequences, these eventualities, they can happen any time."

"All right, all right. Jesus."

"Say it. I have to hear you say it."

"Not ever."

"Not ever what?"

"I will not ever tell Jake about your scam."

"You're a man of honour and a good friend. Be awful to ruin the greatest experience of his life. When we get back, I'll buy you a drink, least I can do. Come on." Howard looked at the falls and sighed. He continued, "You got here at the right time. They'll widen the road first. Then people will start selling drinks. A souvenir stand, a railing, they'll make a viewing point. Developer will open a hotel. Wa will get nothing. They'll get kicked off the land, then the lucky ones will be hired to do an ethnic dancing show. So, come on, let's play happy families."

7

Jake reclined and his girl crouched beside him, fanning him with a big leaf. A picnic was spread out on shopping bags. He said, "We got dumplings, apples, oranges, this weird fruit that I don't even know how to get the skin off of, mango juice, yoghurt, sunflower seeds, peanuts, these things called France bread that are neither French nor breadlike – in fact, they taste like foam – and White Rabbit sweets. I got these 'cause I liked the names." He held up packets of Cashew Savageness nuts and Lonely God crisps. "And three bottles of this stuff." Jake showed a pear-shaped bottle of clear fluid with a bull on the label.

Howard sniffed at it and made a face. "If we run out of petrol, maybe we can stick it in the Jeep." He unwrapped a little foil packet and dabbed prissily at a white powder, licking it off the end of his little finger.

"What's that?" said Jake.

"Yabba. You want a dab?"

"What does it do?"

"It's speed, basically. It's big around here. One of the few manufactured goods coming out of Burma. This is nice, not cut. Here, go on."

"Tastes like hairspray."

"Keep the wrap, there's not much left."

"Will?"

"No, thanks."

Jake said, "Down here, are we in the golden triangle? Where all the heroin is?"

Will watched Howard carefully as he said, "You see any poppy fields? The government leaves the tribals alone only as long as they don't do that. That all happens in Burma. Over the border."

It had occurred to Will to goad the guy a bit – it would not violate the terms of their agreement, and any small discomfort he could cause would be minor payback. "If they're growing it just over the border, there must be a lot of smuggling."

Howard glared at him.

"Yeah," said Jake. "It's not like there're many sources of income. I bet smuggling is huge here. What happens if you get caught, though? Bullet in the back of the head, I bet. I read that. Seems like they'll shoot you for just about anything. Rape, tax evasion, even. You know in the States you can sit on death row for twenty years, having appeals? Guess how long you stay on death row in China? Fifteen minutes. The judge says guilty, they take you round the back of the courthouse, bang. And your family has to pay for the bullet. It's a Confucian thing: if you're a bad man, it's your family's fault 'cause they didn't bring you up right."

"That's an urban myth," said Howard coldly.

Jake warmed to the topic. "Asia is ruthless like that. We met this girl in Hong Kong. Her friend had been locked up in Bangkok. You remember, Will? Sounded like he was having a really shit time. When she visited, they had to talk through a fence, and she tried to give him some books but couldn't fit them through the gap in the wire. And his only crime was to be caught with a little dope in this bag. Sad thing, it wasn't even his bag, least that's what she said. It was his mate's; the poor bloke didn't know anything about it."

"So," said Howard, clearly cutting in to change the topic. "I don't know anything about you guys. What do you do back home?"

"We just finished school," said Will.

"Off to college?"

"He is." Will jerked his head at Jake.

"You?"

"Didn't get the grades."

"I got a college degree." Howard said. "I got an MBA. I'm the maestro of bummer all. An English guy told me that."

"I think you mean 'bugger,'" said Will. "We say 'bugger all'. A master at bugger all."

Howard rolled the word around – "Bugger. Bugger all. Buggering hell" – then put on a cod English accent to say, "Bugger and blast, would you be so kind as to pour a cup of Earl Grey tea. What are you going to do while your friend's off at college?"

Will said, "I was thinking of maybe teaching English somewhere."

"Bottom's fallen out of that market. Time was, you could rock up in Tokyo or Taipei and you'd have a dozen private lessons with doctors and lawyers all lined up and a queue of girls. The chicks would be all, like, 'Wow, you're

a teacher? Will you give me a private lesson in my under-
wear? Will you cum on my tits in English?' It was obscene.
Now that's all gone to shit. Everyone's doing it, the money's crap, and the locals have wised up. They know you're
just a bum who couldn't think of anything else to do. I
really don't recommend it."

"You've done it?"

"One of my many sucky career moves."

"You've lived here a long time?"

"Five years, thereabouts."

"Doing?"

"Living, experiencing, learning. Laying the ground-
work."

"You're American, right?"

"Canadian."

"You miss home?"

"Can't even remember what it's like. I see it on TV
sometimes. It looks fucked up. How did you two end up
travelling together? You been friends for years?"

Jake spoke up. "He grew up next to me. I was planning
to go on my own, but Will said he wanted to come along.
After his girlfriend dumped him."

"She didn't dump me," snapped Will. "Trial separation.
There were issues that needed to be worked out."

Howard gestured at the half-naked girls. "Don't think
this here has got anything to do with that back there. This
is a whole other reality. You understand that, I hope. This
is just this; it doesn't mean more than what it is. So, Will,
how about introducing us to your new friend?"

"I can't get her name right."

"Christen her, then."

Sensing she was being talked about, the girl smiled, then popped a sweet in her mouth, adding the wrapper to a pile at her feet.

"How about Sweet Tooth? Sweetie?"

"I'm calling mine Flower," Jake said, putting his arm around his girl.

"Bet you wish you could take her home." said Howard. He tossed the butt of a cigarette into the pool, stood, and stretched. "I'm going for a swim."

Will's girl followed Howard into the water. Will suspected she wanted to be alone for a while.

Jake caught Will's arm and whispered, "Don't let this slide."

"Huh?"

"You're in. She likes you. I don't know why you're so cold to her. If you don't watch it, the hippie will get in there. Don't let that wrinkly old fucker steal her away. Imagine them together. Imagine how saggy his horrible old arse is. It would be gross. You were getting on all right before, weren't you? I saw you splashing about; you went into that little cave together. So what's the problem now?"

"Just didn't . . . feel right."

"She wants to road-test a roundeye, why not oblige her? You might never get another chance." He patted his girl on the thigh. "It's like the hippie said. Don't make a big deal about it. Go on, be nice to yourself. Go to her."

The girl was a poor swimmer, splashing inefficiently and unwilling to put her head under the surface, and that, more than anything that had happened, made Will think of her as particular and vulnerable. He had already forgotten her name, and he didn't want to think of her as

Sweetie. He said, "I think we should give these girls some money."

"Why? What's that got to do with anything?"

"I think they're very poor."

"They don't want money, they want fun. I'm not saying I buy that crap the hippie spouts, but come on."

Will pointed to the waterfall. "I'm going to get some shots."

Jake pulled him back. "I'm going to tell you something you need to hear. Take that camera off your face. Stop using it like a shield."

"There's a cave behind the waterfall. I'm going to go in there and shoot out through the water. It could work really well."

Jake threw up his hands. "I tried. Don't say I didn't try. But she's going to lose interest soon. Don't say I'm not on your side. I got your back here. You want me to keep the hippie occupied while you make a move, just say the word."

8

Will waded to the waterfall, his camera sheltered under his T-shirt. He clambered over rock, put his head down, thrust through the torrent and scrambled into the cave.

Shooting through the wall of water wasn't practical; the shots would be a blur and, anyway, he didn't want the camera getting wet. He had brought it along only to supply an excuse for the trip. He slipped a hundred-yuan note out of his wallet and tucked it into a crack in the rock. At some point the girls would come to retrieve their knife and watermelon, and find it. They would assume it had fallen out of the wallet earlier and been missed. And, hopefully, the foreign friends would have left by then, so even if they wanted to give it back, they couldn't. They would have no choice but to keep it, with a clear conscience and no sense of having been the recipients of charity. It would brighten up their week. He was sure that the money, less than a tenner in sterling, would make more impact on their lives than it ever could on his.

There was only one thing left to do. Will returned to the beach and coughed until Jake stopped kissing his girl. He said, "I was thinking: how about we walk back?"

"What do you mean?"

"Hike. Through the forest."

"We'd have to leave now to get anywhere civilised by dark."

"That's what I was thinking."

"Leave?" Jake looked at the girl, the sky, the picnic, the pool, each an unspoken argument in his favour.

"Let Howard drive back on his own. I think we should hike back through the forest. It would be a cool thing to do."

"You hate hiking. You didn't even want to do Tiger Leaping Gorge, remember? You were worried we'd get lost, worried about landslides, bandits—"

"I had a good time in the end."

"In the end. And that's a trek that grannies do in high heels. It's marked. Now you want to blunder off into the forest?"

"Yes. I want to walk back."

"Go on, then."

"Yeah but . . . you shouldn't hike alone. It's dangerous. What if I turn an ankle or something? I don't want to be stuck in the forest with a broken leg. So I'd like you to come with me."

The girl had picked up on the sharpness in the voices. She sat back, knees drawn up, arms around them, watching the moving lips.

Jake said, "I'm not tramping through the forest getting hot and sweaty and muddy for no reason. I'm going to chill out here with my new friend, then head back with Howard, and that, frankly, is the winner's option."

"You said that I could decide what we do next. This is me deciding."

"What that agreement was, if a choice comes up between A and B, you make the call. This is not some situation where a choice has risen up. This is you being weird and uptight for no reason."

"I really want to hike back."

"I think you're scared of having a good time."

"I want to do it. And I want you to come with me. As a favour."

"This is typical. Everywhere we go, you manage to have a bad time. I don't know how you do it."

"I have a good time."

"No, you don't, you're miserable. You mope about, you're always watching that stupid film of your stupid ex on your stupid camera. I'm sick of you bringing me down. To be perfectly honest, I wish I'd gone on holiday on my own."

A wasp droned around Will like the personification of Jake's irritation. He swished it away. "I'm sorry you feel that way."

"It's about Jess, isn't it? It's always coming back to her. Get over her. It's like everything you do is this attempt to prove something to her."

"How could that be true? She isn't even here."

"Which makes it doubly pathetic. She called you a wuss, right? Now your whole MO is taking pictures to make albums on fucking Facebook so you can prove to her that you're not – that you're some kind of adventurous spirit. Or, like now, you're thinking about what she'd think if she knew what you were doing, which she never will. Because she doesn't think about you at all."

"She didn't call me a wuss."

"Passive, was that it? Which is a nice way of saying she thinks you're a wuss."

"It was in the heat of the moment and she took it back straight after."

"Well, she was right. You are a wuss. Just . . . get over her. It's over. Move on. Get your ex of your head."

"She's not my ex."

"She is so your ex. She's as ex as ex. I'm sorry, but it's over. She just couldn't bring herself to tell you properly, thought that you might get the hint, might meet someone on holiday, and the whole thing could fizzle out without any drama."

"That's not true."

"She told me. She told everyone. It is over. The only person who doesn't know that is you. You want to know what she's doing now? She's having the time of her life, shagging around like nobody's business. Which is what you should be doing. She's just one of those girls . . . she gives you the full wattage of her attention and those big eyes, and you feel the greatest. But then she moves on. She's like a butterfly flitting about from flower to flower. That's just how she is. Everyone else wises up pretty quickly. I don't know why you haven't." Jake paced to the lake, then back. "She's not worth it. And you know what else? You are well rid. She cheated on you. She was always copping off with other people."

"That's not true. You don't know. How do you know?"

"'Cause there was me. And that's only to start with."

Will blinked hard, and sweat ran down his eyelid into his eye, making him blink again, rapidly. It seemed somehow important not to wipe it away with the back of his hand.

"What?"

"Yes. I did. I'm not proud. I was drunk. We both were. Still . . ."

"You . . . you did that." Will shied away from explicit words.

"The point is, she was going behind your back. Made a habit of it."

"The point is, you copped off with my girlfriend."

"She's not your girlfriend. And she's not going to be your girlfriend again, however many pictures you take."

"Fuck you."

"Okay. Fair enough."

Will turned, not wanting Jake to see his expression, and said as he walked away, "You drive back in Howard's Jeep. You won't see me again."

9

Howard caught up with Will at the bottom of the cliff. "What was that about?"

"Jake will go back with you. But I'm walking. I haven't told him anything, so I haven't broken our understanding. But I'm not going back in that tainted Jeep."

"Tainted? That's a strong word. He's going to think it's odd."

"No, he doesn't suspect. He's very happy with the girl you got him."

"It's dangerous, walking through the forest alone. I really don't advise it."

"The way I see it, it's dangerous riding in your Jeep. I'm not sitting in there like a mug as it goes back through that customs post, no way. I'm not doing it. I'm not, I'm just not."

"If you break an ankle, you're fucked. You might not be found for a week. And there's some pretty fierce people round here. Not everyone wants to be your friend. Some guys, all they going to see is an idiot wearing a suit made of dollar bills. A man can disappear."

"I'm going, I don't care what you say."

"I didn't mention the snakes."

"Now you're clutching at straws. You just want me to carry on playing to your script."

"I'm worried about you. I know what a man looks like who can handle himself in a wilderness scenario, and you don't fit the profile. This is for your sake, not mine."

"I'm going. My mind is made up."

"This is really not a good idea."

"Leave me alone."

"We're going to go back through that customs post, and they're going to wonder how come we're a whitie down."

"Tell them the truth; that I argued with my mate about a girl and rashly decided to walk back."

Will took a couple of steps. Howard grabbed his elbow, and Will shook it off. But the man was only trying to give him a bottle. "You'll need to keep hydrated. If you see a fast-moving stream, fill up, but don't drink from pools. Eventually, you'll get to that village. Better hope you hit another if you miss it. When you do find people, get them to take you to a road, and you'll have to hitch from there. If it gets dark, and you still haven't got anywhere, stop, get comfy, and go to sleep. Don't try and get around at night; you'll just have an accident. Try not to get lost, and don't break a leg. See you for a cold one in town. If you're not back there in three days, I'll get out and look for you. Take care, please."

Will tramped up the cliff. It was good to be looking down at dirt and stones; he didn't want any more beautiful vistas. He walked glumly past the Jeep and onto the track.

Within minutes his T-shirt was stuck to his body with sweat. This track was not taking anything like the shortest route: it was full of tortuous switchbacks. He was vexed to look up and see above him a muddy strip he'd trudged previously. If he had just thrashed through the forest for ten seconds, he would have saved minutes of scrambling around. He realised someone had done exactly that: a path ran straight down the slope. At the next steep downhill, when he saw the track switching back up ahead, he spotted another shortcut through a bamboo grove and took it. He came down a steep slope to a larger track. This was, he assumed, the one they had driven up, but after following it for ten minutes he found it blocked by a fallen tree trunk peppered with fungal breakouts. No vehicle could have come through here. He cursed his stupidity in not spotting the absence of tyre tracks much earlier.

Will started retracing his steps. He decided he didn't like the forest. It was not a vibrant and refreshing cornucopia, full of colour, sensual and lush; on the contrary, it was dark and gloomy, monotonous, sunk in an oppressive perpetual twilight. And the murky green was depressingly silent and deserted – the only evidence of animal life, the flutter and whirr of an unseen bird flying away. There was no shortage of insects, though; the air seemed alive with them. Small motelike things flitted constantly round his face, seeming to be daring one another to fly into his eyes, while others chirruped in the bush, as repetitive and incessant as tinnitus.

He realised that all the mental images he had of the forest, the ones that gave it exotic allure, had been borrowed from TV – and those had been, crucially, shot from above, from helicopters or vantages in the treetops, where the dense canopy could be appreciated for its inhuman scale.

A forest was a thing to rise over and look down at; being in it was dull and uncomfortable.

And lonely. Will was aware of gloomy thoughts that could be kept at bay only when he occupied his mind with present concerns: one foot in front of another, the discomfort of the bag strap pulling on his shoulder, the sweat dripping down his neck, and the chafing of his pants.

After a sweaty and frustrating hour, he found himself at the bottom of a shallow valley, following a stream. A few minutes later, he was thrashing through thickets of head-high grass and, shortly after that, the stream gurgled into a shallow plain of mud and he was confronted by a thicket of thornbushes. It was impossible to go on. It seemed that, once again, infuriatingly, he had gone wrong. He said aloud, "Okay, that's it. I'm lost."

10

It felt good to acknowledge the fact. He was quite calm, though he was aware that a person could at this point start to panic. He told himself that he was not that person. Obviously, it had been rash to take shortcuts. But he couldn't have known the forest was crisscrossed with tracks, that some of them did not lead anywhere but deceitfully dwindled away. Erroneous assumptions had been made, but they had not been unjustified. Well, there was no point in dwelling on should-haves or might-have-beens. What was important right now was to get somewhere he could see farther than his own feet, and not be so insistently pressed in on by plants.

As he trudged disconsolately back, he told himself that the situation was not desperate, merely inconvenient, that he would get out of here eventually, that it was only a question of persistence. If he had to spend the night in the forest, so what? It wouldn't be cold. There was no shortage of water; a person could survive on that alone for a week. He might find trees laden with fruit. Of course, he would be bitten a lot by insects, ravaged. His empty stomach would tighten. The fruit would give him the shits, or he might eat something poisonous. He saw himself walking for days, half-starved, stubbly, dressed in soaking rags. Perhaps, eventually, he would arrive back at this rotten log, and when the realisation came that he had walked in a great pointless circle he would use the last of his strength to howl at the uncaring trees.

He was disappointed with himself for indulging morbid imaginings, and to keep such unhelpful weakness at bay he talked, in rather a hectoring, teachery tone, an idiotic running commentary – "Left foot, right foot; what is that, fungus? Step over the rotting tree, hand on the branch, avoid the sap, what a lot of leaves. What I would really like is a mango smoothie. Careful here: single file, one foot in front of the other, you know the drill . . ."

He stopped when he heard squealing. He didn't know whether to run towards it or away, and, as he dithered, whatever was making it came closer. It was a shrill single note of distress.

11

Leaves rustled, then a black thing hurtled towards him. Only by the glint of an eye could he know it as an animal. He leaped aside and the forest devil, furious panic made flesh, barrelled past, straight and unwavering as a cannonball.

Two skinny figures ran after it. Each held a wooden cross. The elderly man in the lead put a hand on Will's shoulder and gently but firmly moved him aside. Will had time to register worn, pointed elbows and muscles that moved like rope beneath loose skin. The man wore only baggy trousers held up with a rope belt. He was leading a youth, barely into his teens, dressed in a grimy T-shirt and camouflage trousers.

In a moment they were gone. Only as Will got to his feet, blinking at rustling foliage, could he begin to make sense of it. The animal had seemed piggish. That thin adjunct protruding from its flank was an arrow. The men – cousins, presumably, of the girls at the waterfall – were hunting it, and the wooden contraptions they carried were crossbows.

The guys had barely considered him. He was an obstacle. It was disconcerting to be so dismissed. Well, they were busy. They knew he was here. They were moving too fast to follow. Will waited on a broken tree trunk and, in a couple of minutes, they came back.

They were grinning, and the older man carried a dead pig slung over one shoulder, holding it by its back legs, mindless of the blood trickling down his torso, already drying to a crust. In death, it looked much smaller than Will remembered, the size of a terrier. The youth carried the crossbows. Will was glad they had succeeded in killing the pig; he could share in their triumph and admire it. He made a show of examining the thing, appreciating it, then took a photo. Eye contact seemed to make them uncomfortable, so he grew used to focusing his gaze elsewhere on their faces, on the old man's cracked lips and moles, the dimples and acne of the youth.

He showed them the picture on the display. The youth pointed at it, then at himself. Will supposed he wanted a copy. He shook his head. "Can't do that, sorry." He added, "I'm lost," illustrating by scratching his head with his mouth open, feigning exaggerated stupidity and confusion, like a character hamming it up in a silent film. "Maybe you can help me. I need to get to the road." – miming driving a car – "How about you take me to your village?" He pointed at them, at himself, and finished the show by getting his wallet out and showing them some cash.

Will supposed that their lives were as far from his as those of anyone he had ever met. He thought they had a tremendous advantage over him. They were here for a good reason, he for a trivial one, and they knew it, or at least he felt they knew it.

He hoped they wouldn't rob him. It didn't seem likely, but you never could tell. They started talking to each other, and Will watched their mouths, trying to judge meaning from tone. He realised that was hopeless, that about the only thing that could be discerned was the level of earnestness, and he ended up wondering why the young guy's teeth were yellower than the old man's. He realised how nervous and powerless you really were when you didn't know what was being said around you, and it made him think of those two girls, listening to the white folk arguing earlier. Easy to assume the worst.

The old guy beckoned for Will to follow him down the track. He felt relieved but foolish. "I'm glad to see you guys. To be honest, I was getting a bit worried." He didn't want them to think of him as only a stupid lost white guy. He wished he smoked – handing out cigarettes was the only thing he could do that might be of use. He offered to carry one of the bulky crossbows, but the youth waved him away with a grin. They walked in single file, with the older guy leading, and Will at the back making twice as much noise and puffing to keep up. His shoes were so caked with mud they felt like diving boots. His guides, more sensibly, wore flip-flops, and their feet effortlessly found dry and level ground.

Will guessed at their relationship: an old man showing his grandson the traditional ways. As soon as Will had formed that interpretation, their gestures and relationship seemed to come alive to him, and he sought for shots that might capture it. But mostly he caught only the backs of their heads and a green fuzz. They were moving too fast. He looked forward to stopping for a rest. As they thrust on with no sign or intention of stopping, he began to think about asking them to do so. After about an hour of walking, they came to a river and began to walk downstream. Will was very hot and tired, so he didn't even recognise where he was until he saw the Jeep.

The youth gestured at it with a flourish. Will groaned. For over three hours, he had thrashed through the forest, but all that effort had achieved nothing. Misreading his intentions, they had led him right back to the waterfall.

12

Will pretended to be happy, not wishing to disappoint his guides. It was not their fault: his dumb show had been ambiguous, he could as easily have been asking to be returned to his companions. They refused any payment and set off down to the falls, still sprightly, chattering happily. They had hardly broken a sweat. Exhausted, Will curled up in the front passenger seat of the Jeep and fell asleep.

He woke to hear Jake say, "You have touched my heart. I will remember you forever." Through a half-open eye, he watched Jake saying goodbye to his girl in the rear-view mirror. She giggled and pecked him on the cheek. His own girl was there, too. He realised with sadness that he had forgotten her name. Both now wore long black skirts with red horizontal stripes, black tunics, and headbands to keep their slick hair in place. Dressed, they seemed poised, demure. The skirts swirled as they turned, and as they walked away they held the hems up daintily.

Will's T-shirt was still stuck to his back with sweat. The air in the Jeep was close and all the surfaces hot. His neck was stiff, and the mesh pattern of the seat had left red welts on his cheek. As Jake and Howard approached, he closed his eyes again, pretending to sleep.

CHAPTER 12

The back door opened and Jake said, "Oh." He rested a wooden crossbow on the wheel arch and said a guarded "Hey." When Will still didn't say anything, he called over his shoulder, "Will's here."

Will considered Jake through the corner of his eye, imagining him a specimen, a subject to be framed, as Jake said, "I thought you were walking back. What happened? Did you decide against it? Get lost? How did you get all that crap over you? Oh, I see, you're not talking to me." He slid the crossbow along the back seat and got in after it. "I think you're being a bit immature."

Howard got into the front seat, saying, "Good to see you again. I don't mind telling you, I was worried about you tramping off on your own into the forest like that. Glad you saw sense in the end."

Will said, "I asked the tribals to take me to their village. They didn't understand and brought me back."

"Count yourself lucky you got here in time. Imagine if you'd gotten here and we'd already gone. You'd have been fucked. I understand that you and Jake have had some kind of disagreement. I hate to see friends divided, especially over a girl. How about you two agree to a summit meeting when you get back? Get drunk, punch each other out, then make up. Till then, be cool with each other. Can we do that? Agree on a peace pact for at least the duration of the journey?"

"Sure," said Jake. "And Will there's not talking. So, let's go."

Howard started the engine. "How much you pay for the crossbow?"

"I swapped it for those bottles of white spirit."

"Those things take days to make. You got a bargain."

"I got six arrows, too."

"I think you call them quarrels."

"They showed me how to fire it. You have to smear the groove with beeswax, then you pull the string right back, which takes a hell of an effort, then the trigger clicks into position."

"Just don't load it anywhere near me," said Howard. "Those things are lethal. Stronger than a bow. One of those quarrels will go right through you."

"Did you see that pig? Mangled it pretty good."

"Be a pain in the butt to carry round."

"Going to take it apart and send it home. So cool that they actually hunt with these things."

"Not really. They use homemade rifles these days. They do it at night, shine a big light, wait for the animals to come check it out, then pick them off. That was just grandad showing the kid how they did things in his day. You think they found that piglet in the forest, just come across it? No way. They took it from home, let it go and chased it. For the jollies."

"Oh."

Will looked out of the window. How long till the police post? An hour? He knew he would be able to think of nothing else till they were through it. He felt himself a terrible liar and worried that his face alone, glimpsed through a dirty windscreen, would give the game away. He decided that, as they approached, he would pretend to be asleep.

"You had a good time with those girls?" asked Howard.

"I said goodbye to her," said Jake, "and I watched her and her friend walk off into the forest, and she looked back and smiled, and you know what? I wanted to go after her. I really did." He sighed, equal parts wistful regret and satisfaction, then rubbed his jaw. "That stuff, what was it – yabble?"

"Yabba."

"It's quite strong, isn't it? My teeth are sore, I've been grinding so hard."

"A mellow comedown in a café is what you need."

"What is it, really? I mean, chemically?"

"I guess you'd call it methamphetamine. They make it in factories over the border. You'll see it—"

Will spoke up. "Meth? You've been taking meth? Jake, you know what that is?"

"Ah, he speaks," said Jake.

"That's hard drugs, is what I'm saying. I can't believe you've been giving him meth, Howard."

"Not very much."

"It's not like I'm off my tits," said Jake. "If I was off my tits, you would have noticed, wouldn't you? I'm fine. Look how lucid and coherent I am. I can not only remember what the words 'lucid' and 'coherent' mean, but I can use them correctly. Is that the kind of advanced vocab that would be used by someone who is off his tits? What this is like, it's the sober drunk. It makes you super-sharp, very aware. I feel like I could count all the leaves on one of these trees if I wanted to."

Will said, "I heard about being people getting really paranoid—"

"Hey," said Howard. "Set and setting. Don't prime a bad comedown. Forget what he said, Jake; it can be smooth. You just need to get a comfy chair in front of a fan."

Jake frowned at Will. "You're so pissed off all the time. Can't you stop being pissed off? I'm pissed off with you being pissed off all the time, to be honest. Putting a downer on things. I said that, didn't I, Howard? And you think we've just been selfishly enjoying ourselves back there, and you're the martyr, and everyone's out to get you. No. No, it's not true. We've been worried about you, very worried. Couldn't relax at all, for the worrying."

The bout of temper passed quickly, and he started to talk rapidly to himself. "An excellent end to a day that has been memorable and mostly very enjoyable. Mango smoothie, yes. Fan, comfy chair, yes." He chanted it like a mantra: "Comfy chair, fan, mango smoothie, comfy chair, fan, mango smoothie."

The Jeep slowed to round a bend. A motorbike was trundling towards them, ridden by a man in a green uniform. He stopped, kicked the stand down and raised his hand – halt.

Will hoped to see Howard relax, nod, perhaps raise a conceited, knowing little smile – all part of the plan. But he did not. He shifted in his seat, which squeaked. Scanning the track, he frowned and lowered his head. His sudden alertness was alarming. This was not part of the plan.

13

"Comfy chair, fan, mango smoothie. Who's that? Is it a checkpoint?" said Jake.

"It's not a checkpoint," snapped Howard. He stopped the Jeep, looked round, and said, "It'll be fine." The stillness after the engine cut out seemed ponderous. Howard's fingers tapped lightly on the underside of the big steering wheel. Loose white threads at the ragged edges of his cutoffs stood out white against his tanned skin.

Jake groped in his bag. The fabric jerked and twitched. "The yabba," he hissed. "I've still got that wrap. I'd better ditch it. I can't remember where I put it." He rummaged in one zipped compartment, gave up, and moved on to the next. That, too, was no good; he left it and moved on to a third pocket. A pair of socks fell into the footwell. Jake withdrew his hand and shook it to loosen a tangle of headphone leads. "It should be in here, in here, I'm sure it was in here . . . must have slipped down the side."

"Relax," said Howard. "He doesn't care about us. We're civilians. Put the bag down." Then, speaking through gritted teeth, he hissed it again, slower and with more emphasis, like a threat. "Put it down."

The approaching cop was pulling on white gloves. Will recognised him – this was the official who had waved them past on the way here. His uniform was desultory, there wasn't even a hat involved . . . certainly there was nothing special about his bike. The whole weight of his position seemed invested in the gloves; though they weren't standard issue, Will could recall none of the other guards wearing them.

Picking his way towards them between muddy puddles, the man seemed to be moving in slow motion. A spatter of acne ran from the side of his mouth down his chin, making him look young and gauche.

"I've got it," said Jake, his hand stilled in his bag. "I've got the yabba in my hand."

"I told you to leave it," said Howard. His tone was jokey, for the benefit of the cop, but his smile was a grimace. "'Cause it's too late now."

"I'm going to throw it out the window."

"No," said Howard. "Just leave it there." But Jake slid along the back seat. "Stop it," snapped Howard, in a voice so level and tight, it was almost robotic.

Jake took his hand out of the bag and flicked the little foil packet through the open window. Will saw the move and imagined he felt the displaced air. The packet glittered as it arced and it seemed about as discreet as a firework.

Jake said, "It's gone, it's gone." He breathed out slowly.

The cop had seen nothing. He was writing in a notebook. He paused, tapped the pencil on his teeth, looked again at the foreigners, then wrote some more. It seemed he had seen nothing.

CHAPTER 13

"I guess he's writing the numberplate down," said Will.

"Taking his time about it," said Howard. His fingertips drummed a light tattoo on the steering wheel. He muttered, "It's fine. This is fine. Everyone stay calm."

"I don't understand," said Jake. "Why should we not be calm? I ditched the wrap, so . . . What is there to not be calm about? We're clean. Aren't we? Or are we?" He came slowly forward and gripped the front seats. "Howard, are we not clean?"

Howard's fingers froze. "I'm just saying that nobody should panic."

"Why are you saying that?" said Jake. "You're saying that after I ditched the yabba, so why, that's what I want to know. Are we carrying something? Is there something in the Jeep? Is there? Is that it?" Howard continued looking resolutely forward. "You're smuggling," said Jake, clasping and unclasping his hands. "You're smuggling, aren't you. That's it, isn't it? I just want to confirm that's what's going on here."

"Nothing bad is going to happen," said Howard, "because we're foreigners."

"Shit," said Jake. "You are, aren't you? What's in the Jeep? Is it in the boot? Is it? Howard, answer me."

The cop, standing at the side of the Jeep, was waving. The gesture was curt and precise.

Will said, "Howard, I think he wants you to come out. He is going to search the Jeep. That's exactly what he wants to do."

Now that the Jeep wasn't moving, the atmosphere inside had grown close; air seemed a medium that swirled around treacly. What if the worst did happen, thought Will, and their illicit cargo was discovered? Surely Howard would pay the man off. A policeman on his own could be bribed, couldn't he? Though sick with nerves, he was curious to see what would happen, even felt a twinge of enjoyment at Howard's discomfort. He supposed he had more confidence than the other two that this would work out.

Howard opened his door and pushed till it was fully extended. He got out carefully, as if thinking through each movement. He squelched through mud towards the cop.

Jake rocked. Will recalled his own sense of outrage when he had discovered the truth. How much worse to be feeling that in a hot Jeep with a cop right there. "Did you know about this?" Jake asked Will.

"I found out."

Jake licked his lip. "This is fucked." He seemed to draw into himself a moment, then he sprang across the seat divide and plonked down in the driver's seat.

"What are you doing?" Will said. He maintained an odd sense that none of this was quite his concern: he was discovering that, outside familiar grooves, without past experience as a guide, it was very hard to act decisively. The heat seemed to matter, too, as in that drowsy soporific fog coherent thought came slowly. He watched Jake turn the ignition and manipulate the skinny gearstick, and he didn't fully realise what he was up to till it was done: he was simply driving away.

14

The Jeep lurched and hit the cop's bike, knocking it down. Mud spurted, spattering on the windscreen. Will was thrown forward and bumped his head on the side of the door. A searing jab of pain quickly tapered into irritation – what was Jake doing? Now? Here? Really? Why? He directed bad-tempered mental jabs at these stupid people, the stupid heat, the stupid Jeep. When he felt his head, his finger came away sticky. He was bleeding. This was satisfying – the pain was real, the anger justified, there was genuine reason for fogginess and grievance.

The Jeep gathered speed. A thump came from the back. Will turned and saw Howard's face, dark with fury, pressed against the back windscreen. He had jumped onto the boot and clung there, holding on with one hand on the roof, his feet, as they scrambled for purchase, kicking the boot. The cop stood behind, waving his arms.

The track was narrow and bumpy, and branches and twigs slapped the sides. This getaway was a trundle; a man could jog as fast. Still, Will had a sense of things careering out of control. Watching Jake hunched over the steering wheel, and Howard clinging on the back, and in the road behind the receding figure of the cop, he felt himself an extraneous figure, even a little ludicrous, with nothing useful to do or say.

A series of bumps and slaps was Howard manoeuvring on the roof. Will turned in time to see his feet come through the open back window. His legs followed. Howard paused there, wedged precariously, half in and half out, holding onto the roof rack, grunting as branches battered him. With a wriggle, he got his arse in, and his shoes slid along the seat. Like a big fish being landed, he bumped and slid right through the window and onto the back seat. He wriggled upright, pulled his T-shirt down where it had ridden up over his torso, and barked at Jake, "You idiot."

Speaking as much out of a desire to assert himself as to calm the situation, and well aware of it, Will said, "No sign of the cop. Just keep going."

"Yeah, just keep going," said Howard. "Drive on. You fucker. What do you think you're doing? It would have been fine. We could have got through that easy."

Jake said, "Can this thing not go any faster?"

Will said, "Jake, this is maybe not the best idea. That guy's on a bike. A bike'll go much faster than us on a track like this. If he wants, he can catch us."

"We'll just take another road."

Howard threw his hands in the air. "There are no other roads. This is the only way out. We have to rumble along here for an hour, at least, before we find a turnoff. Even then we're fucked, 'cause we're the only foreigners for miles around. We stand out, you know? It's not like it's going to be hard for the cops to find us. And I don't know if you noticed, but he took the fucking licence number." He threw Jake's bag against the door. "Fuck."

"Howard's right," Will said. "We can't just drive away."

"I'm not going to sit still", snapped Jake, "and get arrested for something I didn't do."

"We weren't about to get arrested," said Howard.

The Jeep sideswiped a tree. Will was thrown forward and slapped a palm against the doorframe to brace himself. He had neglected to put his seatbelt on. He told himself to sharpen up; such details were important. When he'd got the belt in place, he was encouraged and calmed by having successfully carried out a sensible, constructive action. It helped clear his head. He said, "We can't carry on. We'll get stopped at some point. So I suggest we dump whatever it is we're carrying in the boot, turn round, and go back there."

"No way," said Jake.

"We go back and explain that you had a panic attack and got a rush of blood to the head. That cop can search us all he likes. It'll look suspicious as hell, but he'll let us off. No choice, 'cause we'll be clean."

Though he was making up the plan as he spoke, as soon as he finished, it seemed the obvious course of action. He could see how it would pan out: they'd return to the policeman and, with curt gestures, he'd order them to come with him. Tedious hours of interrogation would follow, there would be form-filling and harsh words. Fingers would be wagged. Finally, a small fine would be paid, and they would exit chastened and relieved, with a good story. "We have to. I don't care what you're up to, Howard. I just want us to get out of this."

Realising that he would need to convince the others, for the first time in this daft crisis Will felt a sense of urgency. "You dump the cargo. Mark it. Tie that bandana round a tree or something. Then you can get your dodgy friends to come and pick it up later. Or you could come back yourself and pick it up tomorrow. Think about it. Really think about it. We're going to get stopped before we get much farther. Come on, what else can we do?"

Howard drummed his hands against the headrests as he weighed it up. Then he said, "Okay. That's the plan. You heard that, Jake? We stop, dump the load, go back to the cop. The story is, you had a little bit of yabba, and you got scared and drove away, and we – that's me and you, Will – we convinced you that it would be best to go back and confess."

Jake was hunched over the wheel, clutching it so hard that his knuckles whitened, ploughing grimly on. "I'm not telling them I had any yabba. Why should I get in the shit? This is all your fault. You tell them you had it."

Howard tossed a bundled-up pair of socks at him, and they bounced off his head. "You're the one who freaked out and drove off. Why would you do that if I was the one carrying? Sorry, but you have to take the fall."

"Fall?" said Jake. "What kind of fall? Get shot in the back of the head?"

"No, shit," said Howard, "maybe a fine. Not even that, I doubt. Fingers wagged."

"If it's a fine," Will said, trying to be helpful, "we'll all chip in."

"If?" said Jake. "What if it's prison? I'm not going to prison. He should go to prison; he's the one smuggling. You tell them that you were carrying yabba. I'm not co-operating otherwise."

Will said, "We can decide what we're going to say later. We need to stop and get rid of the cargo. Jake, please, stop."

The Jeep came out of a downhill onto a level stretch. A clearing opened up on the left side of the track. Howard slapped Jake's seat. "Go in here."

Will was pleased to see Jake slow the Jeep and turn off. It trundled into scrub and waist-high grass.

"Not too far," said Howard, "or we won't be able to drive out again. This'll do. Stop. Stop." Jake brought the Jeep to a halt.

It was a relief to feel an end to the thump of the suspension and the engine's growl. Will got out into an attractive glade. Any other time he would have reached straight for the camera. Jake was already out and moving. Howard opened the back door, saying, "All right, let's get—"

Jake hurled himself against the door, and it swung hard into Howard. Jake yanked the door, then smacked it back two-handed and this time caught Howard on the thigh. Howard fell forward onto his hands and knees, and Jake kicked him in the stomach. Howard grunted and rolled over with his hands over his face.

Will said, "Hey, hey. Please, come on," and stepped forward to pull Jake away. But the attack was already over.

Howard seemed winded but not badly hurt. Will reached out to help him to his feet, but he batted the hand away.

"Are you all right? Are you bleeding? I got some plasters, if that would help. Shit."

Howard raised a creased face to the sky, as if sunlight would caress the pain away. The violence had diminished him; he looked scrawnier and older. He rose shakily and adjusted his bandana.

Will called, "Jake, that was shit. You didn't have to do that. That really isn't helping."

Jake stepped around the front of the Jeep, aiming the loaded crossbow.

15

"Oh, come on," said Howard. "What is the point of that?"

"Put your hands up. Put them up."

"Get that thing out of my face."

Jake cocked his head to aim along the quarrel. "I said, put your hands up."

"Really? Put my hands up, really? Really put my hands up? That is such a cliché, man. I am very disappointed in you."

"Fucking put your hands up."

"All right, all right. Here is me playing along with your hackneyed scenario. I'm putting my hands in the air like I just don't care. Woo-fucking-woo." Howard put his hands flat on top of his head, fingers interlinked, bony elbows pointing out. "Happy?"

Again Will felt off balance. Perhaps if he were steady, he could get some purchase, but again things had slipped away. He said, "Let's get on with it here."

Jake ignored him. "Where's the contraband?"

"Con-tra-band," said Howard. "What command of the English language. Can tell you're a college boy."

"Stop messing around."

"It's in the boot," Will said. "I'll dump it now." He took a couple of sideways steps, happy to get a bit of distance from the crossbow's glare.

"Leave it there," said Jake. "We're going to tie him up, put him in the Jeep, get back to civilisation, and tell them everything. Everything. It's the only way."

A wasp landed on Will's cheek. Brushing it away, he realised his face was slick with sweat. "I'm not sure that's a good idea."

"That is a very bad idea," said Howard. "Me, I'm nothing, you don't need to be scared of me. But you don't want to piss off the people I'm working for. They're scary people. I'm scared of them. They don't give a fuck about anything or anyone. Kill you soon as . . . Don't mess with these people."

Will gestured at Howard. "I don't like this guy, either. I don't like the way he duped us. But we can't prove that we weren't in on this. Let's do what we'd planned: just get rid of whatever's in the Jeep and go back to the cop."

"No, we're going to tie him up, get back to civilisation, and tell them everything. It is the sensible option."

Howard said, "I really didn't want to do this, but you've forced me into it. I have to tell you what I told Will earlier. Anything happens to me, if I get arrested or handed over to the police or anything like that, those lovely little girls that you were playing with are going to get into a lot of trouble."

"Yeah, yeah," said Jake, "make your empty threats."

"Those girls were paid to keep you out of the way. The people who own them are horrible. I'm telling you: anything happens to me, and those girls will pay for it. Shit, they'll probably get killed."

"You're lying."

Will said, "I'm not sure he's lying about that, Jake."

"Of course he would say that; he'd say anything."

"Take your finger off the trigger," said Howard. He was standing very stiffly, but his elbows wiggled back and forth. "You're making me nervous. Can you do that? Lay your finger along the side of the trigger, not on it."

Jake's trigger finger stayed where it was. "Will, tie him. There's some cable under the back seat. Tie his wrists together behind his back. His ankles, as well, and tie his wrists to his ankles."

Will said, "I really don't think it's such a good idea."

Howard said, "There is no point in tying me up. That is a terrible plan." He took a step forward. "Stop pointing that fucking thing at me."

"Stop moving or I'll shoot you," said Jake.

"You'll shoot me? Really? You'll shoot another human being? You'd do that? You are in a rut here, and I think you need to step out of it right now and look with objectivity at where you are and what you are doing, because the further you head down this road, the harder it is to get back, and you will want to get back, believe me, you will."

"I will shoot you in the fucking face. Will, tie him up."

Howard hissed, "If you shoot, you'd better kill me, 'cause if you don't, I'll kill you. Only one shot in that thing. You could easily miss. Or just graze me, a little flesh wound there – ouch, it smarts. Your hands are shaking. Awkward, isn't it? Heavy. Look at you. Hard to keep steady. You could miss. Then you'd learn what trouble is. I'll be coming right at you, no mercy. I'll show you how to fight dirty. I'll show you how a dirty fighter fights."

"Will, tie him."

Howard shouted, "Stop pointing that fucking thing at me."

Will went to the Jeep. The striped cable curled in the footwell was about a centimetre thick and several metres long. With both guys out of sight, it occurred to him that if there were something clever to do, now would be the time to do it. It would be nice to have a plan; he would feel less humiliated and anxious. But he could think of nothing.

When he came back round the bonnet, the problem still had the same shape: two guys, a crossbow. But now a butterfly, farcically conspicuous with its metallic blue wings, fluttered towards one man, then the other, as if drawn to the charge between them. They ignored it, and of course he should, too. He said, "Howard, I'm going to tie your hands. Put them behind your back, please. Jake, point that thing away. I'm not tying him up until it's pointed away."

Jake lowered the crossbow a little, aiming at Howard's feet. Howard put his arms behind his back, and Will began to wrap the cable round them. "Make sure it's tight," said Jake.

Will had not tied anyone up since games of cowboys and Indians as a kid. He remembered his mother stopping him, warning of the drastic effects of cut-off circulation. The memory made this scenario feel unreal, like playacting. He secured the cable with a set of granny knots, one on top of another. The whole situation was like that: an ugly mass of tight little knots making a mess that would take some unpicking.

"Turn him around," said Jake. "Show me. Okay, good. Now his ankles. You have to tie his wrists to his ankles."

"Howard," Will said, "you'll have to lie down on your side for me to do this. Put your ankles together and bend your knees."

"Careful," said Jake. "Don't let him run away." The tip of his tongue protruded from between his lips.

"He's not going anywhere, is he?"

Howard shifted and carefully lay on his side, and Will wrapped the cable around his ankles. "We should carry on with the original plan." Will spoke as much for his own benefit as anyone else's, pleased to hear his calm, reasonable tone. "Yes, I'll tie him up, but I don't think it's the best idea. I think that we might have a problem proving to the cops that we weren't involved in any of it, and I believe Howard's right that those girls will suffer if we continue down this road."

Will grew aware that there was something stilted about his delivery, and he had a strange urge to laugh, which vanished when he looked up and glimpsed the crossbow. Jake's arms shook with the effort of keeping it raised. With the string tense, the thing seemed a creature in its own right, kept in check only with difficulty. It was like something holding its breath; eventual release seemed inevitable. Will leaned away from its gaze.

"That's not good enough," said Jake. "You need to get more around his ankles."

"There's not enough."

"Is there any more in the Jeep?"

"No."

"You used too much of it on his wrists. What's that? Granny knots? Come on – you don't need that many. Unpick some and do it again."

"Well, you know what they say," called Howard. "If you want something done properly, do it yourself." Then he whispered to Will, "It's true what I said about the girls. He won't listen to me. Make him see sense."

Will finished his knots and stood. Howard stayed down in the grass, where he was barely visible. Not being aimed at emboldened Will, and he said, "I think we should carry on with the original plan. I'm going to dump the stuff out of the Jeep."

"No," said Jake. "We're going to take it to the cops, along with Howard."

"We don't know what we're messing with. We're in a foreign country, and we don't know the score at all. Maybe the cops have been paid off. Maybe we'll end up upsetting some dangerous people. And maybe those girls will get in trouble, like he said. Come on, think about it. They were too good to be true."

"Jess had you nailed right. You just want to play it safe, it's all you ever do. This guy's a sleazebag, and he used us, and he needs to be punished. Show some spine."

Will shrugged. "All right. Look. I don't know. You've got the crossbow. Your call."

"Put him in the Jeep."

Will grew aware of a droning sound. At first it seemed another addition to the incessant insect chorus, but as it got louder and more distinct he realised what it was: an approaching engine. Jake's eyes flicked right and left, then, as if in entreaty, up at the heavens. Howard got onto his knees and glared. They all knew what it meant: here was the policeman, puttering after the villains on his little bike.

16

Once again, it seemed, a huge mistake had been made. They should have driven farther and concealed themselves properly in the trees. It surely would have been worth the risk of not being able to get back to the road.

Will said, "Shhh. Everyone be quiet."

If they could ditch the contraband – Jake's old-fashioned word seemed appropriate now – it wouldn't matter whether they were seen. But the boot was locked, the keys still in the ignition; he wouldn't get it done in time.

"Shit," said Howard. "Stay down, everyone, stay down."

Will and Jake crouched. Will supposed they were thinking the same thing: if they were found by the police now, they could not claim ignorance. Having Howard tied up didn't make much difference either way; they looked guilty as hell.

Listening to that swelling buzz, Will could picture the cop clearly, puttering bravely forward, but what he might be thinking was a mystery. Perhaps he was very annoyed that his bike had been knocked over. Maybe it was dented, and if they offered to pay for the repair, everything would be all right. Or maybe he was angling for a bribe. Perhaps he was only baffled and hurt and wanted an explanation.

Or perhaps he burned with a righteous fury to bring smugglers to justice.

The bike came alongside, and Will longed for the engine noise to start dimming as the man trundled on. But it didn't. It cut out.

Will exhaled slowly. That was it – no escape. They just had to sit here and hope he didn't see them. And if the cop found them, what then? It was easier to think without having to look at Jake and the crossbow. They would be arrested, taken to a town, interrogated. Will determined to tell the truth as soon as he found someone who could understand him. There would be a great deal of inconvenience, but he was, after all, completely innocent, and surely that would become clear in time. There was every reason for optimism.

Whatever Will told himself, his stomach tightened with nerves. He felt the impulse to see what was happening and did not fight it hard enough. Though aware that it was an unnecessary risk, he peeked.

The cop was off his bike, looking thoughtfully down. He was studying the tyre tracks. They should have made an effort to conceal them, it was so obvious now – another failure.

Grass swished as the cop approached. He came upon the scene and stopped. Will saw him take in the little drama: the Jeep, Howard on his knees with his hands and ankles tied, Jake toting a crossbow. They looked like Will felt: furtive, awkward and embarrassed.

Jake said, "We're not smugglers."

Howard said, "Get your cash out. You, too, Will. We're going to have to give him all our money."

"He's a smuggler," shouted Jake. "Him. Not us." The crossbow shifted. Will suspected that he was not more than half aware of it, the thing pointed where he looked. The cop made urgent palm-down gestures – put it down, put it down.

"We have to bribe him," shouted Howard. "Show him money."

"He's a smuggler," said Jake. "We tied him up because—" The crossbow discharged with a sigh. The cop took a step backwards and groped at his chest. A crossbow quarrel was embedded there. Will had not seen it fly; there had been no crunchy noise of impact. It could as easily have grown out of him as been driven in.

The cop opened his mouth as if to speak, then closed it again. He touched the quarrel with two fingers, delicately, then the thumb joined them. The thing seemed set firmly in there. He put both hands on it, but they seemed pale and uncertain things compared to the vigour of that hard bolt, and they weakened further, and lost what certainty they had, and fluttered and dropped. The cop fell to his knees. Blood was flowing gently down his shirt. He keeled neatly over onto his side and became a dark shape in the grass.

"Oh, fuck," said Howard.

Will couldn't make sense of the cop being there like that. He didn't seem quite real any more; it was as if he had been superimposed.

The body repelled and attracted in equal measure. The man lay with one hand across his chest, lightly holding the crossbow shaft. His face held an expression of slack-jawed dismay as his eyes moved rapidly, taking in, Will supposed, last impressions: the green void of leaves, pale alien faces. They looked at the sky and settled, and the shallow breath faded. Will whispered, "You shot him." It needed to be said before it could be believed.

Jake approached, coming at the body slowly and taking it in in glances, as if its awfulness could not be confronted all at once. The crossbow fell from his shaking hands. "I didn't . . ." he said, and tailed off. He looked away, then back, perhaps hoping the scene would miraculously change from one glance to the next. Will wanted that, too, wanted the man to stand up, brush himself down, and tell them it was okay, they were not so far from home as they thought.

"Is he?" said Jake.

"Yeah," said Howard.

"Definitely?"

"Yes, he's definitely dead."

"How do you know?"

"He's got a fucking arrow in his chest. You've killed a cop." There was wonder in Howard's tone, an awed appreciation of the event as spectacle – it wasn't every day. Will supposed that, if he could, Howard would be rubbing his bristly chin in that way he had.

"It was an accident."

"I know. You accidentally shot him in the heart with a crossbow."

"I'm telling you, it was an accident."

"It's a shame. It's still murder."

Jake was pinching his lower lip between his finger and thumb. "Oh, Jesus."

They ignored Will as completely as if they were acting out a play and he were the audience. Which suited him fine. The body, the smuggler, the shooter – it seemed a tri-angle, neat and self-contained, a drama with no role for him. He took a careful step back, removing himself further.

"I want a cigarette," said Howard. "There's a packet in my pocket. If you're not going to untie me, will you light one for me? The left pocket. There's a lighter, too."

Will was surprised to see Jake obey, but perhaps, at a complete loss, he was pleased to have a task to perform. His hands didn't shake as he lit a cigarette and slotted it into the corner of Howard's mouth.

Howard puffed with his head tilted at an angle and one eye closed, to avoid the sting of rising smoke. It was the kind of face, Will noted, that you'd pull if you wanted to look like a jaunty pirate. He was aware that it was hardly a helpful observation, but that presence on the ground sabotaged thought, and his mind kept catching on irrel-evant details – the serrated edge of a leaf, a shaggy creeper curling round a trunk, the way the texture of the tyres mirrored with the bark of a tree.

Jake came towards Will, holding out the soft pack of Stone Forests. He had been included and must now, how-ever unwilling, play a part. "What are you doing?" said Will. "You know I don't smoke."

"Would seem a good time to start, I'd say." Jake took Will's arm, leaned in, and whispered, "Let's say Howard did it. Let's go up the road in the Jeep and find the other cops and get across – how, I don't know, with diagrams or something – that Howard did it. No one can prove other-wise. He's the smuggler. What do you say?"

17

Will considered taking a cigarette just to delay having to answer.

"Well?"

He said carefully, "I didn't shoot anyone, I didn't smuggle anything, I just . . ." He trailed off. Just what? Just didn't want to be involved.

Jake's grip tightened. "Let's say he was threatening us because we found out about the smuggling, and then the cop came, and Howard panicked and shot him, and then we knocked him down and took the crossbow and tied him up. It makes sense. You have to admit it makes sense."

Jake's story clearly pleased him. He would tell it, Will was sure, very convincingly. It was neat, and the truth was cluttered.

The hand gripping his arm was warm and sweaty. Will looked down at it, and Jake let go and wiped his palm on his T-shirt. His fingers had left faint red marks on Will's skin.

"It's not much of a stretch," said Jake. "They'll believe us. We get the story straight and then stick to it. I should think they'll only ask a couple of times."

He waved his hand, and the proffered cigarette fell into the grass. They looked dumbly down at it. "I'm really sorry to put you in this position. I really am. If I didn't think it was totally necessary, I wouldn't ask. It's a big favour."

Jake licked his lips. "Come on, Will. It won't be difficult. Who will they believe: one smuggler or two innocent tourists?"

Will imagined himself saying yes, and the word swelled in the space behind his lips. After all, it was only a syllable, and it would end this awkward scene. A new kind of journey would begin as soon as that noise was made, an uncomfortable trudge full of awkwardness and inconvenience, but with a definite goal. Keeping to the story under questioning would require great nerve and concentration. He could see himself in a police interrogation room being stared at by fat cops. He had never been in a Chinese police station, or met any policemen, yet this mental picture was surprisingly vivid. Nothing on the table but a telephone and mugs of green tea and a red-lined pad. The mildewed wall was painted green. The translator, the only person not in uniform, repeated, "It does not make sense. How did Mister Howard have time to load the crossbow? Why didn't you stop him?"

Will realised that most of the details of this picture came from watching ten seconds of a Chinese soap opera on a hotel TV, and that led to another image. He saw himself lying on a hotel bed, watching the Chinese news. The pretty newsreader was replaced by a shot of a courtroom, and there was Howard, his hands shackled, standing in the dock flanked by policemen. One was pushing his head down. Howard's head had been shaved, and looked as pale, round and fragile as a lightbulb. Here the image veered from naturalism, because, as in a dream, he could understand the voice-over without worrying how: this murderer was being sentenced to death.

He shook his head and said with genuine sadness, "I can't."

"You what? But you can, you can."

Will felt suddenly irritated and wished that this earnest person with damp hands and serious concerns would get out of his face. "No, I can't."

"You mean you won't."

"All right. I won't."

Jake briefly folded his lower lip under his upper teeth, then stared fiercely into Will's eyes and held his gaze. Will could see a glimmer of his own distorted reflection in the pupils. "I know it's a lot to ask. Please look into your heart and find it in yourself to help a friend in need."

"Sorry."

"We've been through a lot together."

"I know."

"And I understand that I might not be your favourite person, especially at the moment, and that you feel that you own me no favours. However—"

"I can't."

"You keep saying that, but you can; that's exactly what you can do. It's a case of us having a story, then getting it straight." Jake ran a hand through hair damp with sweat. "There's no point in saying I . . . there's no point in saying I shot him, because that isn't what happened. I mean, that's what happened, but it isn't what really happened, it's not the truth of it. It was an accident, I didn't mean to. It was the same as if the guy had been killed by a coconut falling out of a tree, or a rockslide or a snakebite or something, 'cause it was just a thing that happened. It was a – there was no intention – there was no intention there. It happened because of the situation. And the situation was caused by Howard. He's the person whose fault it all is. Howard. It's his fault. So there's a kind of justice in saying it was him." Jake let his hands drift down his face, then put his palms together in an attitude of prayer, with the fingers pointing at Will. "Is he or is he not a fucker?"

"Yes."

"Has he screwed us over? Has he ripped us off?"

"Yes."

"Has he broken the law?"

"Yes."

"Should he be punished?"

"Yes."

"There it is, then." Jake opened his hands. "Help me out. Come on. It's just a favour for a mate who's in a sticky spot. One that will not be forgotten."

Will felt shamed, as if he were the supplicant. He began to reply, but the words petered out – "Um, but, I . . ."

Jake, in contrast, seemed to have found a rich vein of rhetoric and continued talking rapidly. "All right, look. I know it's a lot to ask, I know, so in consideration of the effort involved, I'll get you that new camera you've been banging on about. When we get back to Hong Kong, I swear, I will get you a fantastic camera. A beautiful machine."

That made it easier. Will didn't need to consider it for a moment. If he did what was asked, it would be as a favour; to do it for a price was corrupt. He said, "No," and shook his head, and felt sorry for his friend.

"All right. You want it now. I can give you a grand right now. You don't have to wait. I've got travellers' cheques. I can sign them and give them to you. Then you can take them to any bank and cash them."

"No."

"A grand right now, in your hand, and a camera when we get to Hong Kong. It's the easiest money you'll ever make. It's a simple job of work, we both win, and that fucker goes to prison."

"He wouldn't go to prison, though, would he? He'd be executed. And I can't . . . I can't be responsible for killing someone, I just can't."

"So you think I should be executed? I should die now? You want me to die?"

"I didn't say that. I didn't . . . Sorry, but if I get asked what happened, I'll have to say what I saw. Sorry. Maybe you can convince them it was an accident. You convinced me. They'll test the trigger, and see how light it is, and then . . ." He was unable to give any conviction to what he realised was a pretty poor argument, and his voice dwindled away again. He was aware of a stupid childish urge to wave his hands, screw up his face and wail.

"I told you I copped off with your girlfriend and now you want to kill me. That's it, right?"

"No, come on."

Jake balled his hands, unwittingly crushing the cigarette packet. "I don't want to get executed. What's the use? What's the point? You're actually going to kill me. For no reason at all." He shook with frustration. "No, you do have a reason. You hate me, don't you? You've always hated me. You hate me and now this is your chance. You're enjoying it. You're loving this." He screwed his eyes shut, and the cigarette packet rustled as he crushed it. Then he opened his eyes and he had stopped shaking. The angry frown had gone, but red blushes had appeared high on his cheeks. "Okay, forget I said that, forget it. I'm understandably stressed out and I'll say anything."

He spread his hands in entreaty and the packet dropped. It lay in the grass, the foil top sparkling. It was a pretty thing, and Will wanted to keep looking at it. But Jake got down on his knees, covering it.

"This is me in my hour of need, begging for help."

Will shook his head. "I said no. Please get up."

Jake sat back on his heels. "I don't want to die."

"I said, if I get asked. I didn't say I'd go to the cops. I didn't say I'd actively do anything against you."

"Look at me on my knees here. I'm down on my knees to you here."

A cough made them both turn. Howard stood with his legs wide apart, aiming the loaded crossbow. He said, "And you can stay there."

18

Howard jammed the butt of the machine into his shoulder and took his hand off the trigger to show his palm. A pocketknife glimmered there, a stubby blade with a wide base and a bone handle held in place by his thumb. The cable coiled at his feet.

"Always keep a blade on you. I learned that from the tribals. I had it in my hand, then I slipped it in my back pocket when I put my hands behind my back, and it didn't take long to get through the cruddy rope. See how resourceful I am? That should be a lesson. I'm not a guy you want to be up against."

He slid the knife into his pocket, then put the hand back up and laid his finger alongside the trigger. He looked relaxed, and he moved and spoke with slow deliberation and didn't blink much, and Will couldn't help thinking that, as he had said, he was a man you wanted on your side.

"Will, keep your hands in front where I can see them. I liked your spirit there, camera boy. The man is a camera. Camera doesn't lie."

Jake glanced aside, and what he was thinking was written on his face – he wanted to run. He had to take only four paces before being obscured in thick brush. But with a crossbow swivelling to find his back, they would be a very long four paces.

"Don't do it, lover boy," warned Howard. "I've only got one shot, but it'll be a good one. I'm not going to miss from here. I just want to talk. Let's talk. Okay?"

"Okay," said Jake, but shifted his weight onto one knee and squatted like a runner – ready, if necessary, to bolt.

Will said, "Sure."

"Let's look at this, really look at it – leaving aside, for the moment, issues of blame and responsibility, none of which is helpful at this point. We have a pretty picture, don't we? A couple of things strike me. That unfortunate little fellow, he's short and dark. He's not Han; he's a minority, almost certainly Wa, like the other little fellows round here. That's very unlucky for us. Means we can't have any locals stumbling into this. 'Cause tribal justice, it's not subtle. These people don't fuck about. Lynch first and ask questions later. Locals get hold of us, they'll kill us all."

"So?" said Jake. His voice had a hectoring edge, and he didn't sound to Will like a man who had been pleading for his life seconds before. Perhaps he was anxious to assert himself.

"Let me finish. Over and above that we have Chinese law – I mean the actual written law of this fine nation – cops and courts might be a bit more interested in establishing who did what to whom, but I'd say not much more. And we all know the penalties for murder under Chinese law."

"Stop saying that," said Jake. "Stop talking about it like that. It was an accident."

"What does it matter? Who cares? That doesn't alter any facts."

Will said, "Is there not a chance that if we explained—" He stopped. The word 'explained' seemed risible as soon as it was out.

"I get the impression", said Howard, "that you have this idea that, 'cause nothing here is your fault, you'll be all right, you're a civilian sitting on the sidelines with the camera. Is that what you're thinking?"

"No."

"Because that analysis is very wrong. This is our problem. His problem, my problem, your problem. You're not in England. You think the people who come in and find this mess, you think they're going to listen to reason? You think they're going to take statements, carefully put it all together? Find out who knew what, who was taken for a ride, who was riding whom? Dust for fingerprints, use a laser to work out the path of the fatal blow, like on *CSI*? No way, man. One of them got fucking shot. And we're a gang of arrogant white fuckheads; white people, yeah, you know the kind, pasty fuckers who started the opium war and walk round the planet like they own it. They will kill us. If this gets out, we are dead. All three of us. I don't like it, either. I didn't shoot him, did I?" He pointed. "That shot cop is going to be the death of all three of us. Unless. Unless, unless. Unless we act together, fast, now. I am accepting the reality of this fucked-up situation, which you are not."

"So . . . you want to drive off?" said Jake almost perkily. "We should just drive away? You're catching on. We're going to try and get away with this."

Will said carefully and slowly, "I think you're only saying that 'cause you're a smuggler." He was looking up so he could see Howard and the crossbow only through his peripheral vision, knowing that considering either directly might make him falter. Still, his tongue felt thick in his mouth as he said, "And any kind of investigation is going to turn up your racket."

"Okay, if you're going to be like that. You're going to be the good witness, the truth-teller, Mr Camera. So maybe you'll go to the cops and say Howard's a smuggler and young Jake here shot a cop."

Will looked straight at Howard. The man was smiling pleasantly; they could have been shooting the shit in a bar. "But let's carry that scenario further. Imagine me and Jake, maybe we'll be there, too, and we'll say hang on, no no no, see that Will there, he's the smuggler, and he shot the cop. Where does that leave you? Two guys are pointing the finger, and you're only one guy saying things were any different. How does that sound to you, Jake? That sound like something not outside the bounds of possibility?"

"Well . . ."

"Well, he says. That's an interesting well, a well that says a lot. That's a well that says I am open to possibilities, I could be persuaded. That's the well at the beginning of a road. So I'm going to save us a bit of time and take it as a yes. See how it is now, Will? Your friend here is no slave to truth. In the scenario recently outlined, you'd be the one getting fucked over. I'm not saying that's going to happen, understand, just sketching possibilities. What it comes down to, it doesn't really matter who shot the cop. Or who was smuggling, or who knew what about it. We're all screwed if this gets out, me and you and him, all of us, fucked up equally and equally fucked. Which leaves us with only the sensible course of action. And Jake knows what that is, don't you, Jake?"

"Let's get out."

"Jake's behind it. That just leaves you, Will."

Will realised how precarious his position was. He supposed Howard's threat was a genuine one – if they were captured and it came to witness statements and the whole tedious unpicking of cops and courts, then yes, he could see Howard and Jake banding together to ensure that he, Will, was blamed. There was enough in it for both of them, and they had the solidarity of sinners. Even say they weren't caught – Howard and Jake could not trust him, could they? As far as they were concerned, they would be safer if he were dead. He was in more trouble than anyone else. He did not know quite how it had happened, but it seemed he had stumbled into very dangerous territory.

Will closed his eyes and heard Jake say, "What's wrong with him?"

"Give him a moment," said Howard.

Red light pulsed on the inside of Will's eyelids. He told himself he was going to make it work out, it was all going to be fine, he was going to work hard for as long as it took until it was all right again. He opened his eyes and found the crossbow, Howard, Jake, and he took the measure of each of these points of interest. "Okay." He wiped sweat off his face with his T-shirt and said "Okay" again, louder this time, an assertion of his presence.

"Okay, you're with us on this? Say it."

"Okay, yes. I am with you."

"There you go. A band of brothers. Stand or fall together."

Will looked down, wanting to see the dead man again, to consider the size and shape of the problem. But the dead man wasn't there.

19

Where the cop had lain was a patch of flattened, blood-flecked grass. For a moment Will entertained the fantasy that the man had never existed and the last few minutes, so unbelievable anyway, had been a temporary rupture, now repaired. He had to remind himself that, no, the man had been here and had been shot. Now he could see a trail of blood spatters.

Jake followed his gaze and said, "Oh, shit."

Howard came over. "Fucker's crawled off."

Will said, "This changes it." This thing could perhaps be retreated from. "He's still alive, so that changes it. We have to find him and take him to a hospital."

Howard shook his head sadly. "No hospital can save him. Not round here. And say it does – no one can save us. He's going to tell a story about how we drove away from him, then shot him. That's the death penalty for sure. We have to find him and finish him. It comes down to mathematics. One dies so that three survive. Three is a bigger number than one. That's the end of any debate you think might be worth having at this point."

Will's head swayed, on no conscious instruction. His heartbeat was so fast, it felt like some creature in his chest was trying to kick its way out. Sweat prickled on his fore-head. He had an odd idea to cool himself as a dog did, by opening his mouth. The forest moved: full of glittering edges and points, it seemed to be closing in. The sun beat angrily down, splinters of light reflected off the windows of the Jeep. He ran. There was no notion behind it but a need to be elsewhere.

Howard yelled, "Stop him," then something thumped into his thighs and knocked him sprawling. He lay winded. Jake had tackled him. He rolled over and saw Howard aiming the crossbow at his chest. He was looking straight down the line of the quarrel at a squinting eye.

Howard said, "You're not going anywhere."

Will lay still. Howard said, "Jake, tie him up."

"What about the—"

"The cop can't get far," said Howard. "He's bleeding heavily. This first. Tie him to the Jeep."

"Why?" Jake asked.

"He's not getting with the programme. Don't know what he might try next. It's for his own good."

Jake gathered up the cable. He looked aside as he mut-tered, "You heard. Go over to the Jeep and put your hands behind your back."

Will sat on the back seat with his hands behind him, and Jake crouched beside the half-open door and lashed his wrists to the door handle. Will kept thinking of things he wanted to say, then deciding it was better not to say them. It occurred to him that Howard and Jake had forgot-ten their real target, and the source of discord, and were directing their confusion and anger at him. Perhaps they wanted to forget. Even this thought did not seem worth expression. He did not care so much about the man they were intending to kill; he was too worried about himself.

Howard addressed Will. "That was a dumb move, soldier. We need you to show some clarity here. Either you're with us or you're dead. I think we've established that both me and Jake are absolutely one hundred and ten per cent serious when it comes to it. So you'd better play along, camera."

There was a new sharpness in Jake's voice as he said, "Howard's right. You just can't face it."

"I don't like it," said Howard. "I didn't shoot the little fellow either."

Jake closed the Jeep door, and Will winced as the cable cut into his wrists. Through the open window, he watched Jake stand and say, "Well." It sounded absurd, but then almost anything would.

Howard held the crossbow out to Jake. "He's not going to be hard to find."

"What do you mean?"

"You know what has to be done. Go and do it."

"What?"

"Go and do the guy."

"Well, I—"

"Go in there and shoot him, and get it right this time. You'd better aim for the head. Make it pop like a watermelon."

"I . . ." Jake's syllable trailed off into a croak.

"You don't want to? I just heard you say that was what needed doing. We've agreed. Fuck. Now what?" Howard walked away, out of view, then returned rubbing his chin. "I'll do it. I'll go and do what has to be done."

"You will?"

"Yeah."

"Thank you."

"For the money I heard mentioned in a previous context."

"What?"

"You tried to give it to Will a couple of minutes ago. I believe it was a grand. Correct me if I'm wrong, but that's your quaint parlance for a thousand pounds sterling, is it not?"

"Well, yes. Wait a minute."

"Okay, you do it."

"Shit."

"The guy is crawling away. We're losing valuable time while you fuck about here."

"But you said—"

"You're asking me to kill someone. A grand is pretty inexpensive. You know what a professional would charge?"

"Okay, okay." Jake unzipped his money belt and withdrew a dog-eared envelope. "A thousand pounds in travellers' cheques. Take it."

Howard said, "They'll need to be countersigned."

"I'll do it later."

"You'll do it now. Pen?"

"In the Jeep. Can we not do this later?"

"No." Howard aimed down at an imaginary target on the ground a couple of metres ahead. He gave a soft plosive breath. "Poosh." He was showing them what it would be like to kill a wounded man. "Go and get it."

Jake went around the back of the Jeep and opened the door opposite Will. Will glared at him as he fished among his stuff. He spotted the pen in the footwell and put his trainer over it. But it was no good; he just felt like a wilfully obstructive kid.

Jake picked up his bag, turned it over, and shook it. Chewing gum and sunscreen fell out. He pushed Will's foot aside and snatched the pen up. Will kicked his arm but couldn't get much weight behind it. Jake slithered out and slammed the door.

Howard said to him, "I'm not moving till all those cheques are signed."

"How do I know that you'll—"

"Every second he gets further away."

Jake flattened a cheque on the Jeep bonnet. "This is money from my dad. 'Just for emergency,' he said. 'Use it only if you're in trouble.'"

"He'd understand, then, because this is you in trouble. We never know what's going to happen on holiday, do we? That's a lot of the excitement. Getting into scrapes, meeting strange new people, fucking them, shooting them." Howard picked up the cheque. "Your handwriting's fucked. No bank'll take that. Get a grip. It's your own signature – surely you can get that right."

Jake signed cheques, and Howard folded them and put them in his pocket. There was no rush. Jake seemed, if not pleased, at least glad to be active. It was not a particularly unhappy scene: it went on for what felt to Will like a long time.

Howard said, "Who gets travellers' cheques in twentypound denominations? You couldn't get five hundreds?"

"Make it quick. I want it to be all right."

"We all do, Jake. It's harsh, but it's the right thing to do. There isn't an animal in this forest that wouldn't understand." Howard put away the last cheque and laid a hand on Jake's shoulder. "This will definitely make you feel better – I was going to do it anyway."

Howard slunk off, studying the ground, taking big, careful strides, and was soon gone into the bush.

Jake leaned back against the bonnet. He said, "Fuck. Fuck. Fuck." Then he said, "Shut up."

"I didn't say anything," said Will. Perhaps the cop would get away. Will was only mildly interested, as if he had a small bet on the outcome. Perhaps it was because he'd thought the guy dead once already, or perhaps it was the heat. He imagined getting away – anywhere would do.

"I'm not stupid. I know he's a fucking psychopath." Jake walked once around the clearing, taking big heavy strides. When he came back, he said, "Will?"

"What?"

"This is fucked up."

"I know."

"I've never seen a fuckup like this. I've never even read about a fuckup like this. I'm going to have a cigarette. I'm going to start smoking. I tried it before, but I think I never gave it a proper chance." He found the discarded packet and took one out with shaking fingers. "You haven't got a light, have you? No, why would you? Doesn't matter, there's one lying on the dashboard."

He got the cigarette lit, inhaled, exhaled, coughed. "I wish I was where you are. I really do. But I had to . . . I had to stand up. I had to face it, and I did. And you didn't. You ran away. Still. I wish I was where you are."

"How's the cigarette?"

"Rancid. I wish I wasn't . . . I'm still speeding like crazy. That stuff is really strong. It's not a little pick-you-up at all, it's a fucking . . . It's raging through me." Jake held up the smouldering cigarette and regarded the tip intensely, giving the illusion that his concentration was making it burn. "The thing is, the thing now is, it's about getting out. It's, there is no bigger picture. It's just this. It's this. In a straight line." He appeared to be addressing the cigarette. "You're always . . . you go round, you got to stop going around. This is this is this. It's about what's in front, it's about the right steps. The steps which are . . . necessary. An animal. It's about flesh and blood and being, being an animal, being a thing which wants, which needs, to go forward, to go on. To continue."

Will glimpsed movement in the rear view mirror. It was a momentary shadow, and whatever made it had gone when he looked across.

"I'm talking total shit. What am I saying? I don't know. I've got a joke – do you want to hear it? No, well, anyway. Blue tarmac and red tarmac are having a drink, right, and green tarmac comes into the bar and he orders a drink, a shot, and he drinks it in one gulp, and then he punches the barman in the face. Blue tarmac turns to red tarmac and he says, "You've got to watch out for him. He's a fucking cycle path.'"

Jake dabbed the burning end of the cigarette against the back of his hand, and flinched as it burned. He blew on the ember to get it glowing red, then pressed again, much harder, mashing it into his flesh. "Ow. Fucker."

Jake flicked the broken cigarette away, then spat on the burn. Waving his hand in the air, he said, "Congratulations.

You're the good guy. I would love to be where you are now. I would love it. But someone has to have the balls to do what has to be done. I wonder if you're as good as you think. You're glad, really, secretly. You're glad that we're doing what has to be done."

Something had changed on the back window on the blind side of the Jeep, and it took a moment for Will to register what. The tips of four fingers rested on the window base. The gloves were not pristine any more; there was a smudge of dirt at the end of each fingertip. Will imagined the hand, then the person: the injured cop was squatting beside the door. Will almost smiled at the unexpectedness of it.

20

Will said, "I'll tell you a joke." His idea was to keep Jake's attention; the man should not see the cop. He was sure of that, though not quite sure why. Perhaps it was a form of advantage that he didn't want to lose. He didn't have a joke handy, and groped for one. "Okay, well, uh, there's these two chimps in the bath, and one says to the other, 'Hoo hoo hoo hoo!'"

Mimicking the chimp, he realised that an edge of hysteria had entered his voice. He let it come because it seemed to give cover to the babbling, but now that it was here he didn't seem able to dislodge it. "And the other one says, 'Put some cold in, then.'"

"I told you that," said Jake.

The swish of grass distracted Jake, and he turned. The cop reared over him, a stone held with both hands above his head. His face was pale, and his lips drawn back in pain. From the centre of a dark stain on his chest, the crossbow bolt pointed, rude and accusing.

The stone thumped down on Jake's head. He took a step back, swinging his arms uselessly, then crumpled, landing with a gasp. Blood dribbled down his cheek. He lay on his elbows and knees with the broad curve of his back presented to the man, his T-shirt stretched tight over the bobbles of his spine, and Will thought, If he hits him again, it might kill him.

Then it occurred to Will that he might be next. He pulled his arms back in the futile hope of tearing off the door handle. The plastic rattled, and a ring of pain gripped his wrists.

Earth clung to one side of the rock, moss to another. The cop panted. His face was in shadow, but a splinter of sunlight caught his side and illuminated the dirt on his arm and a split seam in his shirt. A quivering began in his hands and spread quickly down his arms. Will watched strength and purpose leak away.

The man swayed and dropped the rock. He took a stiff forward step. A bloody palm slapped the driver's window, then slid across it. His eyes met Will's. Will hauled again at his bonds, felt them tug him back, and thought at the man, See? I'm a prisoner. If the cop did not see him as an ally, at least Will could raise doubt over his status as an enemy. The eyes slid away as quickly as if Will had been inanimate. Clearly, the man was not going to waste any energy on him.

He groped along the Jeep as if hauling himself along a ship's deck, opened the driver's door, got into the seat and turned the ignition. Every movement was like a first unpractised attempt. He appeared to have some difficulty getting the gearstick into reverse – perhaps he wasn't depressing the clutch properly or the shift was tight – and Will urged him on: "Get us out of here."

The cop wrapped both hands over the gear knob and leaned until it ground into place. Then he lay back and panted. The back of his neck was pale, and sweat stood out on it. A hand came up to lightly grip the shaft of the crossbow, as if in wonder at its continuing presence there. It was in him, tight and unwavering. He settled himself and gripped the wheel.

Will admired his fierce will. What determination it must have taken to play dead like that, to wait till the whities were distracted and hide, finally to come out and steal the Jeep. All with an arrow burning in his chest.

The cop turned and looked out the back window, and his eyes did not register Will's presence at all. Above the rumble of the engine was a sound like a bicycle pump. It took Will a few moments to realise it was the man's breath, expelled rapidly between gritted teeth.

The Jeep bumped slowly backwards. He was trying to take it to the road.

Will said, "Untie me, please. I'll drive. I'll drive you to a hospital, I promise. Untie me."

He tried to remember his few words of Chinese. "*Ni hao. Ni hao. Ni hao.*" 'Friend', what was 'friend'? A girl had taught him. *Ping? Pang?* She had been selling flags to celebrate National Day, she was bored and hungry, they went to a KFC, she told him the flags had been her mother's idea and she just wanted to play on this the day when the Chinese had stood up. To his surprise, she had paid for the meal – *peng you.* "*Peng you,*" Will shouted. "*Peng you.*"

Twigs and leaves batted the bodywork. There was a way back to the track, but this wasn't it. The cop was taking them into a tangle of bushes.

"Please, please, *ni hao, ni hao, peng you,* let me drive. *Tai gui le.*" It was the only other thing Will could say in

Chinese; he shouted it out of frustration and a need to be understood. It meant 'that's too expensive'.

The Jeep bumped back against a tree and stopped.

"Let me drive. Free me and I'll drive."

A few metres in front of them, Jake was getting groggily to his feet. He stood, feet wide apart, swaying as if the earth were moving. He dabbed at his wound with his fingers, then looked at them in consternation, like he was annoyed that they had got so dirty.

The cop grunted, leaned forward, and got both hands around the gearstick. He moved with his chest thrust out, as if being pulled by the crossbow shaft. As he moved, more blood bubbled from the wound. The crossbow bolt looked so absurd, protruding like an emblem. As he weakened, it seemed to grow stronger. With great care, he ground the gearstick into first, then settled back into the seat.

He revved the engine. As soon as he took his foot off the clutch, the Jeep would rush forward, right into Jake.

"No, no," said Will. "Don't run him over. Ignore him." Will slithered down and forward and got both his feet over the handbrake and through the front-seat divide. The rope cut into his wrists. Just as the cop let the clutch go, Will snaked a foot into the gap inside the steering wheel. With a wrench, he turned it aside. The Jeep lurched forward, turned sharply, missing Jake by inches, then crashed into a bush. There was a great thrashing of leaves, then it hit a tree trunk, and came to rest.

"Okay, great. Now reverse. We'll get out of here. Or, or, just come back here and untie me, please. Come and untie me. I'll drive."

An odd hiatus stretched; it seemed that minutes passed. The cop sat back, breathing heavily. He waved his hands in a lazy arc, then one arm settled on Will's outstretched leg. Will could smell the man's blood and breath. Slowly, delicately, as if trying not to wake an entwined sleeper, Will got his foot out of the wheel and retreated by inches to his place on the back seat. He could see the cop's face in the rear view mirror. It had stiffened into an expression of resigned disappointment.

Will realised that he was watching the man die and that the process was messy and sad and undramatic. He felt a strange unmooring of the senses. He could see, but was unable to put a name to anything. Details – the patterns on the seat and the writing on the corner of the window – crowded his attention and seemed as important as anything else. All he could hear was a ringing quietness, as if his fellow traveller were sucking all sound with him as he went.

Sometime later – impossible to tell how long – noise began again with the clunk of the driver's door opening. The body of the cop slithered out sideways, leaving a foot resting on the front seat.

Jake and Howard peered down.

Jake said, "Is he?"

Howard prodded. "Yeah. This time. Yeah."

21

"Tough son of a bitch, wasn't he?" Howard addressed the troublesome corpse. "Idiot. If you'd just waved us on, you'd be alive now." He pointed at the crossbow bolt. "Look at this. The arrow went through the notebook in his shirt pocket. That slowed it down."

Howard pressed one hand flat on the man's chest and pushed down as he hauled on the quarrel with the other hand. As the bolt came jerkily out, fresh blood flowed from the wound. It ran in rivulets between his fingers, then ebbed darkly away into the saturated shirt. The bolt slid up and free, painted red.

Howard pulled out the dead man's notebook. Droplets of blood ran off the glossy plastic cover. The quarrel had entered near the bottom corner and punched a ragged hole right through it. Delicately, he separated and turned the pages and said, "There's English in here."

He showed Will. Above an uneven bloody tidemark, the paper shone shockingly white. Chinese characters were written in pencil in a fastidious hand, and next to each was an English word, painstaking and alone, in unjoined small case: *sky*, *cloud*, *car*, *pear*. It was a vocabulary list.

Will said, "He didn't say anything to us."

"Was working up to it."

"You think that's why he stopped us? He just wanted to practise his English?"

Howard flicked on past more pages of vocabulary. A single phrase was on the last page. The cop had written: *I hope you like our waterfall.*

"Guy rode all that way just to talk to some foreigners. Probably been learning for years and never got a chance to practise."

Will could imagine how their conversation would have gone: *Where are you from? How do you like my country? What is your name? Are you married?* That was how it should have been: simple, forgettable. To fuck up such an ordinary thing was as ridiculous as it was tragic.

"He just wanted to talk to us . . ." said Will. "Then this is all pretty stupid."

"In retrospect," said Howard, "it was pretty fucking avoidable."

They had done well, Will thought, at maintaining a sober, sensible tone. It was shattered by a wail from Jake. "Fuck. He's dead." He seemed to roll the syllable around, sampling its dusty taste on his palate. "Dead."

Howard grabbed him by the shoulders. "That's just man-shaped meat. A problem, not a person. Look at me. Shit like this happens all the time; we're just unlucky that it's happened to us. We are going to be all right. But we need to be strong. We've climbed onto the dark horse. And the dark horse, once you're on it, you have to stay on it all the way, as far as it takes you – and sometimes it takes you a long way – before you come out into the light. If you stop or you haven't got the guts to carry on, you're fucked. The people who never get on the dark horse, they're fine. They live their little lives, they're civilians. And the people who can ride the dark horse as far as it wants to take them, they're fine, too. The people who fuck up are the ones who get on the dark horse and try to get off before it's done with them. All I am is a guy who does what needs to be done. I know the dark horse, I recognise it, and I know how to ride it. And we, all three of us, are going to ride it all the way until it delivers us into the light. I promise you that. You hear me? I promise you. Stick with your uncle Howard, and you'll be okay." He hugged Jake. "You understand?"

"Yes."

"Good lad. I think Will understands, too. So the first thing we are going to do is untie him."

"He'll run away, or . . . We don't know what he'll do."

"I don't think so," said Howard. "Yes, it's his first impulse. But then he's thought it through. It has occurred to him that if he does take off, maybe those two – that's me and you, Jake – will get themselves out of here with a cooked-up story about how camera boy lost his shit and killed a cop with a crossbow. And he's going to be thinking, Well, there's two of them, there's only one of me here denying it, and no proof of anything either way. So that's worried him. So then he's thought, Well, if I can't leave, what can I do? And he's coming up with no solutions except the one he hates. The only thing he doesn't want to do is the only thing he can do."

"What's that?" said Jake.

"Cooperate. We none of us have any option but to stick together. At least till we're safe. Then we don't ever have to see each other again. Will, do you see how it is?"

"We're in the forest."

"Good man."

Howard opened the door behind Will and untied him. As soon as he was free, Will got out, desperate to be away from that hot metal box with its blood stench. The insects continued to buzz like ringtones, the sun to shine. He waved away wasps. Maybe the blood was attracting them. There was blood all over his hands, even under his fingernails. He knelt in the grass and tried to rub it off and succeeded only in smearing it up his arms.

"All right," said Jake. "Let's go."

Howard said, "We have to hide the body."

"We can drag it into the bush."

"He's going to smell. Animals will start on him. Plus, when he doesn't go back to the customs post, the other cops will start a search party. Could be he'll get discovered in a day or two."

"So what?"

"They'll find a body that's been shot with a crossbow. We bought a crossbow – that'll get out. They know where we were, when, and that the guy was coming to meet us to practise his English. It looks pretty bad."

"They won't be able to prove anything. Will they?"

"They might try."

"But . . . It doesn't matter. They won't be able to find us. We can just leave the country."

"You can. But I have to live here. And let me make something clear. If they finger me, I'll give them you."

"Well," said Jake, shifting his feet, "you don't know who we are. You don't know our surnames. You told him your full name, Will?"

"No."

"I haven't, either. So . . ."

Howard shook his head and sighed the way a man playing chess might chide an opponent for a dumb move. "You're both signed in to the Bamboo guesthouse, right? Remember those forms you filled when you checked in? Name, passport number, visa number . . . those get stored at the police station. All they need is a first name, the name of the hotel, and the date you stayed there, and they got you. So it doesn't matter where you are, a beach in Bangkok or a college in London: if they want you, they'll come for you. And if I get busted, I'll make sure they come for you. Bet on it. Just saying, no offence meant. So." He tapped the sole of the dead man's shoe lightly with his foot. "We can't let this problem get found. Not at all. Not ever. With no body, there's only a missing person. If it gets to murder, and they realise he was shot, things will get very uncomfortable. For all three of us."

Will said, "Take him to the river." He had not intended to whisper, but that was how it came out. He coughed and raised his voice to say, "It's that or bury him, and we don't have a shovel. Rope, we've got. We can weigh him down with his bike."

22

"All right," said Howard. "We'll take him back. It's only about a ten-minute drive. Load him into the Jeep. We'll put him on the back seat." But nobody moved.

"Close his eyes," said Jake.

"You do it."

"I don't want to touch him. I mean, I'll help you pick him up, sure, but I don't want to touch his skin."

"Pretty squeamish for a killer."

Howard closed the man's eyes, then took the legs, and Jake and Will grabbed an arm each. He was not so heavy, but he was disconcertingly warm. Will kept noticing details that marked him as individual and particular – cracked skin on his elbows, a patch of what might be eczema on his wrist – and each was a rebuke. There was even something uncomfortably specific about his uniform – a badly repaired seam to his trousers, laces tied with a double knot. All this, this accumulation of detail that was a person, it was all pointless, would all be wasted. Will grew aware of alleys of thought that could be gone down that would make him unable to continue, and he realised the truth of Howard's words. The man had to be treated as a problem of a particular weight and size; anything more, and clarity of thought and action was impossible.

They got him through the back door of the Jeep and slid him along the seat. It was so easy, it felt like he was co-operating. Will wanted the man to get up and tell them that what they were doing was the only thing that made sense in the situation. Perhaps he could give them some pointers on this strange territory they had blundered into. But Howard slung the crossbow in and shut the door on him.

"I'll ride the bike," said Jake, and Will followed Howard into the Jeep.

"Stay focused," said Howard as they set off, "and we are going to win."

"There's no winner. This is not a game."

"Of course it's a game. It's just a serious one."

"It's murder."

"You think I'm a robot? I'm all heart. I cry when a puppy hurts its paw. But given the choice between nursing an uneasy conscience in a hammock on a beach or in a cell, getting my arse creamed to butter, I pick the leisure option."

Jake followed a couple of metres behind, revving the bike hard, his jaw set in a grimace. Will wondered if he, too, was replaying the incident in his head and this time getting it right. It was merely a shameful list of errors that had led them to this sorrowful position; there had been nothing ordained or inevitable about any of it. What a vast array of ifs Jake would have to consider – if he hadn't driven away, if the crossbow's trigger had been stiffer, if he had never met Howard or never left home.

Will grew aware of what seemed a great variety of cuts and bruises and sore points on his body, few of which he could trace to a source. His wrists smarted from the rope, but where had the pain in his fingers come from? The ache on his temple – was that when he bumped his head during the drive or during the ride with the wounded cop? All these scars on his arms – how long had they been there? He hoped they were from thorns rather than fingernails.

His mouth was dry. There was a bottle of water in his bag, but he didn't want to get it out, as then he'd have to give some to Howard, and he didn't want the man's saliva getting on the rim of a bottle that he might later want to drink from himself. He wanted nothing of that man in him.

It struck him that these disjointed thoughts were inappropriate. Did it indicate some fundamental moral flaw to be so concerned with his own body when the issue, so plainly, was with someone else's? Of course, it was impossible to know what was normal or fitting at a time like this. Perhaps fatigue, pain and stress had made him more animal.

The Jeep came to a long level stretch of track. Up ahead, two dark figures sat cross-legged.

Howard groaned and stopped the Jeep. "Who the hell?"

"It's the crossbow guys," said Will.

"What are they doing?"

"Just hanging out, it looks like. Maybe hunting, waiting for prey. I don't know."

"They shouldn't be here. They weren't there ten minutes ago." He thumped the steering wheel. "This track has been deserted every other time I've been up it. Now it's a fucking highway. Where did they come from?"

"What do you want to do?" said Will. "You want to go back?"

"I don't know. I don't know."

Behind them, Jake had pulled up on the bike. "What is it?" he called.

"And you can shut up," said Howard under his breath. "This is very bad for us." He was eyeing the crossbow lying on top of the body on the back seat. "This dark horse is taking us far."

"No way," whispered Will. His fingertips pressed into the flesh above his knees.

"I'm just not ruling out any options." Howard rubbed his chin, pulling the flesh of his neck so that it tightened over his jaw. And finally it occurred to Will why he did this: the gesture had begun as vanity, to tauten sagging skin, and become habit. "We can't have witnesses – you know it."

Will peered harder through the mud-spattered windscreen. "They're not moving. They're just sitting there."

"What is this, a rotary meeting? Haven't they got homes?"

The younger guy lurched, his head swayed, and he put a hand down to stop himself from toppling over. Granddad threw his head back and laughed, and for a moment his teeth flashed and his tongue darted quickly.

Will said, "Jake paid for the crossbow with booze, right? So that's it. They're pissed. That's what going on here. They're having a party. They're stumbling round, drunk."

"However much they've drunk, they're going to notice, remember. We can't trundle past them like a funeral procession. A dead cop is not an insignificant detail."

The two men stood.

"I think they've seen us."

"They're going to come and say hello."

Will gripped Howard's arm. "I'll get them to shift."

"How?"

"I'll do it. Relax. Don't worry about it. Stay there. It'll be fine."

"Why should you go?"

"'Cause I know them best, don't I?"

"You're covered in blood."

Will took off his T-shirt and shorts and left the Jeep dressed in his boxers. Jake came up and said, "Why are they here? I thought they went home. What are you getting undressed for?"

Will felt assured as he said, "It's fine, I'm going to get them away. It's fine."

"How?"

"Go sit on the bike."

The level tone and quiet confidence had achieved their objective, which was to keep Howard away from the crossbow. But Will had no idea what he was going to do. For a few paces, he savoured being out of his tainted clothes; he knew he wouldn't be putting them back on. He hurried towards the men, and without even thinking about it, because it was what he would do normally, he opened his bag and got his camera out.

He felt the thing lent him legitimacy: he was not just a dirty blundering wild man, he was a man with a camera, here to make a record.

"Hey, guys."

The grandfather held a half-empty bottle and took elaborate precautions not to spill any as he unfolded knobbly limbs and rose. The lad bounced to his feet and chuckled. They seemed genuinely pleased to see him, slapping his back with drunken bonhomie. The old man tapped the bulge in Will's boxers and gave him a thumbs-up, presumably congratulating him on the size of his packet. His grandson held mollifying hands up to Will, while, it seemed, slurrily berating the old man – telling him off for a perceived breach of social convention. When the lad addressed Will, he knew exactly what the kid was saying: You know what old folk are like, he's being friendly, don't think anything of it.

Will waved their apologies away. The old man thrust the bottle at him and Will pretended not to see it. "So," said Will, and a pause hung in the buzzing air. "I was thinking you might want to come with me to have a little photo shoot in the forest." He tapped the camera, and became awkwardly aware of his muddy, bloody hands. "Come on, guys. Come in here." Will filled his voice with enthusiasm; he reminded himself of a children's TV presenter. He skipped a few paces into the bushes, gesturing with the camera for them to follow, but they just stood and watched. An observer would think that he was the drunk one. "Come on guys, help me out here. A portrait. Jungle hunters in their natural environment kind of thing. The sun coming down through the leaves. It'll look great. I'll send you a copy."

The old man lowered himself into a squat and sighed as he fixed himself into place.

The youth followed his lead. The dead pig lay in the crook of a branch; the crossbow was propped against the trunk.

Will's shoulders sagged, and he gave in to exasperation. "Otherwise you are going to get shot. You are going to get shot by the fucking psycho in the Jeep over there."

23

Will looked back down the track. The bonnet poked out from a backdrop of greenery like the snout of a watching predator. The light was behind it, so the windscreen was dark, and he could not see Howard. But he imagined him in there stringing the crossbow, muttering about horses, his eyes dead.

"So, come in here. Please?"

Now the youth took the bottle and waved it. Two empties were stored in his thigh pockets: this bottle was their last. Drunk, his delicate features were slurred into a dopey grin and his face was very red. Perhaps this was the first time he had ever got drunk: he had gone out to learn something with his grandad and received a different and unexpected lesson. Well, it was certainly a day for that.

Will took the bottle and swigged. The acrid liquid went down with a punishing burn, then exploded in his chest. Convulsing, he was aware of the old man's eyes following the open bottleneck – he did not want any spilled. The bottle – that was the answer. Will screwed the cap on, then turned and thrashed into the forest. As hoped, the guys headed in after him, calling in bafflement. Thorns scratched his shins as he blundered. It wasn't long before the old man caught up with him, put an arm around his waist, and, puzzled, started asking questions.

Will said, "I'm sorry about this."

Will heard the rumble of the Jeep, and the buzz of the bike. They had taken this opportunity, now that the path was clear, and headed along the track. Will hoped they had not abandoned him.

The young guy was gesticulating, slim hands fluttering about his head. Will tossed the bottle away. It clinked and rolled in the undergrowth, but he didn't think it broke.

The guys frowned at him, and held their hands up in entreaty. What could be the meaning of such a pointless act of cruelty? Then the old man tut-tutted, in exactly the way Will's grandmother did, before trudging away to look for the bottle.

Will ran after the Jeep. It had not gone far and, when he appeared, stopped. Getting in felt like a dirty and disreputable move. "I don't like this," said Howard. "Not at all."

"They're totally pissed, they've gone, let's go. Let's go."

"What did you do?"

"Threw their booze into a bush. They'll be in there for a while, looking for it."

"You're not their favourite person any more, then. You don't want to see them again. They can be an unpredictable bunch, especially when they're drunk." Howard gave a short, harsh laugh. "But you know what? That was a good move, camera. You're going to be fine."

This little success brought Will a sardonic flicker of satisfaction, and following it came a sense that this situation could be retreated from, that the damage could be limited and controlled, that normality could once again be possible. But when they stopped above the waterfall, Will's mood dipped. Travelling, he was passively accomplishing something, but now he had to be active, and confront the ugliness anew. He stood at the cliff edge, looking down. It was still a beautiful place, thrillingly alive. "It's deep there," said Jake, pointing. "I dived down far as I could – three or four metres, easily – and didn't see the bottom."

Will pictured their cop lying down there in the dark. He would bloat with gases. Fish would nibble him away. Bones would settle in the silt. The bike would maintain its integrity for much longer. Yes, it was a good place to put a body.

Howard was tugging the corpse off the back seat, gripping the arms just above the shoulders. The cop came down slithering, then folded up and lay curled like a sleeper, one hand resting on his chest and the other thrown out casually, palm up. The head lolled, exposing a dark and bruised neck. How had that happened, and why? There would be many more changes, of course. Will was glad they would soon be rid of him.

Jake said, "Got to get this bike down there. We could just throw it off."

"No," said Howard, "it'll break apart. Evidence will break off and bounce all over the scene. It has to be wheeled down."

"I'll do it," said Will.

"You could barely get down there on your own, let alone wheeling a bike."

"It's my turn for the bike. I want to do it."

"I'll manage," said Jake.

"The stink of blood in that Jeep was so bad I nearly threw up. You fired the shot. Go and help Howard with . . . " Will paused; it was taboo to give the body mental shape. 'It' seemed too cold and 'him', bringing to mind the humanity the man had lost, too painful.

"Let him do the bike if he wants," snapped Howard. "It's his turn."

"You go first," said Will. "It's going to be dangerous if I'm close behind you. I could drop the bike, and it would fall and hit you. I'll wait till you've got to the bottom."

"All right."

Howard was on the arms, Jake on the legs. Howard stepped onto the path, looking over his shoulder. Jake waddled behind him. Both men seemed engrossed in their distasteful task. In a few seconds they were out of sight.

Will opened his penknife and reached into his bag. It was a good bag, canvas and double-stitched, but there was a hole in the side. With the knife, he worked the stitching loose and widened the rip with his fingers. He set the camera on video and wedged it in the bag with the lens aimed through the hole, and packed it in tightly with his books and clothes. There. Not a bad job. Even if the visual did not catch the action well, the microphone would pick up the dialogue.

Howard called up, "Will, what are you doing? Get that bike down here."

"Coming."

Will wasn't quite sure what he intended to achieve with this hidden recording, but he thought it might give him options if this thing didn't pan out as hoped. Howard and Jake, it seemed, would not hesitate to lie, so perhaps a weapon could be made of truth.

Will put the strap around his shoulder and tightened the buckle to keep the bag fast under his arm, with the hidden lens directed forward. Hopefully, they were so used to seeing the bag that they would not question why he carried it now.

Howard and Jake were almost at the beach. Howard was at the front, holding the dead man's ankles. Jake shuffled awkwardly behind, holding the arms. As Will watched, the man's shirt snagged on a bush, and Jake let go of one arm to free it. The body twisted sideways, causing Howard to stumble, and he let go. The dead man rolled off the path, arms windmilling, and fell feet-first into a bush, which bent under the weight. Then the upper torso rose like a man waking and pitched forward, and the corpse turned a somersault and slid face-first down a patch of scree. From there it bounced and landed on the path near the bottom of the cliff. Howard and Jake hurried after it, and Will turned his face away.

The bike was a cheap model, with a light frame and thick tyres. Even this was not safe: the warm exhaust pipe, the sweaty handlebars, and a gash in the seat repaired with red wire, all brought its owner uncomfortably to mind. On the straights, Will trundled and bumped it recklessly down. He enjoyed feeling it start to slide out of his control, then snatching it back again at the latest possible moment; it was an expression of his frustrations. The switchbacks were too tight to steer around, so he had to pick the clunky thing up and swing it round on its side. But he did not mind: it felt like a kind of proper work, and he was glad to be getting smothered in grease. It was covering the bloodstains.

24

Howard and Jake had the body laid out on a flat rock that jutted out above the pool. The cop was a horrible thing that just got more grotesque, and each new wound seemed a shameful violation. He had been broken in the fall: his shoulder was hunched right up level with his chin, and one leg bent unnaturally underneath him. It seemed as terrible as anything else that such a posture didn't pain him. Loose lips and a slack mouth gave him a moronic expression. His eyes were open again. One was cloudy where it had been poked by a branch, but the other was wide and shockingly clear; it seemed to be taking everything in with equanimity. Will lay the bike down beside the body and scuttled out of the path of that interested gaze.

Howard said, "We need to get him tied to the bike. It'll hold him down. We'll throw him off the overhang here."

Will turned, and the bag swung, giving the camera a sweeping panorama. He hoped the automatic focusing was catching the scene and not trying to focus on the scrap of material that half obscured the lens. Enunciating clearly for the benefit of the hidden microphone, he said, "I wasn't the one who shot him. You can do it."

"That's not the helpful attitude we're looking for," said Howard. "I'm disappointed."

"So shoot me, too."

Will went to sit in the shade and laid the bag beside his thigh with one hand over it so that he could aim the camera. Jake and Howard started tying the dead man to the bike, trussing him with cable, working hard, losing themselves in the simple task.

"You could help," said Jake to Will.

"I'm not touching the thing."

"You touched him before."

"And never again. I already played my part."

During his time away, whenever he confronted a scene that seemed particularly exotic, Will had been conjuring a mental gallery of approving Jessicas to note how far he had come. Now, as he watched the cop being trussed, the gallery came unbidden, only this time the Jessicas were alarmed and dismayed, saying, "There's no coming back from this," "Your life will never be the same" and, most powerfully, one incredulous voice that kept repeating, "A dead body, right there, a dead body."

Will paced in a circle to make the voices go away, then, acutely conscious of the weight of the bag pulling at his shoulder, took a deep breath and approached the scene. The dead man was strapped along the bike with his knees tied to the back wheel, his arms embracing the front. His expression was as bland as the sky. There was little now in common with how Will had seen him when alive. He was a parody, and anything could be done to him. They could cut the body, fuck it; none of it would count. After one taboo had been broken, all others became thinkable.

A record of the event didn't feel like such a good idea now. It seemed a childish act of rebellion, motivated by petulance as much as anything else. Well, it was too late; the plan was in place, and to try and stop it was riskier than going on. In his mind's eye, Will saw the semicircle of black holes on the camera body, the microphone, as he said, "Did you really have to kill him? I mean, I can see that we have to hide the body, you've given us no choice, but . . . Did you really have to kill him?" He thought as he repeated himself that he had overdone it. Howard and Jake looked at him coldly. Yes, he had gone too far. Howard knew what he was doing and now perhaps would kill him, too. But the man said only, "It had to be done."

Will hoped the machine had caught that. He felt the way he had when pushing the bike down the path, recklessness creating giddy excitement. "I'm not convinced, there must have been something—"

"There was nothing," snapped Howard. "We've been over this."

Jake secured the cop's wrists with a cluster of knots, stood, and wiped his hands on his trousers. Howard was letting air out of the tyres.

"Let's just get him in," said Jake. "We'll push the thing off, okay? And you can help Will. Come on."

Howard pulled the handlebars, and Jake and Will pushed a wheel each. Metal scraped stone, and the bike slid without fuss over the edge. Will heard but didn't see the thing go into the water. When Will stepped up, there were only ripples to look at. He imagined the thing settling in the silt far below, welcomed by weedy tendrils.

Watching ripples spread then subside, he grew conscious of a shared intensity. A body consigned to blackness – even for murderers, it was a poignant moment, a time for prayer or reflection.

They turned away, enjoying a few seconds of relief. The period of maximum mess had passed; this was surely the start of things getting neater. For a moment they were a band, and Will, as the traitor in their midst, felt a twinge of shame at his deceit.

"We're filthy," said Howard. "Come on." He ran around rocks to the beach and waded hard into the water, and as soon as it was up to his torso he launched himself under. He came up, shook hair out of his eyes, and ducked again.

Will laid his bag down on a rock at the side of the pool, aiming the camera aside, towards the waterfall, wanting to keep it out of the way now that it had done its job. The water soothed, and he appreciated the cold flare as it reached his balls. He dropped under the surface into an attractive, simple place of merciful dark and the bubbling roar of white noise, and he left it as long as he could before coming up for air.

Jake said, "Hey, Will, haven't you got some soap?" He was naked and walking unhurriedly towards the bag, picking his way across stones on the balls of his feet, arms spread for balance.

In alarm, Will raised his hands to his head and turned the gesture into a nonchalant one by slicking his wet hair back. "No," he said, trying to keep his voice under control.

Jake said, "Sure, you packed your washbag, don't you remember? Mind if I—" He was fumbling with a metal buckle. It glimmered as he moved it back and forth. Will watched, powerless and despairing, as the bag was opened and a hand went in.

25

In a moment Will's subterfuge would be discovered. He decided he would tell the truth, lay it all out. He would explain that he had no specific plan, just wanted reassurance – after all, had they not threatened to tell the cops that it was all his fault? And if that unlikely event were to come to pass, it would be good to have a record that proved otherwise. There was no malicious purpose, surely they could see that? There had been no thought of going to the cops with any recording. Neither had there been considerations of blackmail or extortion. It was a stupid thing to do, yes, that was accepted, and of course it didn't look good. Had they not all done stupid things today? Watching Jake's delving arm, he felt the sentences form, and opening his mouth to begin his explanation he shouted, "Snake!"

It was the result of no conscious thought. It was just a bark with all his anguish in it, and it shocked Will nearly as much as Jake.

Jake jerked upright. "Snake!" Will yelled again. "Snake, right there," and pointed randomly with a rigid arm.

Jake stood in place, legs planted wide, head moving rapidly as he looked round. "Where?"

Will waded hard out of the water. "Don't move, don't move. Right there, stay right where you are." The more panicky he sounded, the more he was selling the story, and it felt easy and natural to gush on. "Don't move. Don't move." A cruel part of him was even amused.

"I can't see it."

Will bent to peer fiercely at innocent rocks. Presently, sighing with feigned relief, he let his shoulders sag. "I think it's gone."

"Really?"

"It was there." Will chose a suitable surface for his glittery-eyed, tongue-darting phantom to bask on. "Its head was up and swaying" – he demonstrated with his hand – "and I thought, shit, it's definitely going to bite you."

"Just there?"

"Just there."

They contemplated this marvellous escape. "Maybe it wanted to go for a swim and you were in the way." Will shook his head. "I really thought it was going to go for you."

"What colour was it?"

"Black and red."

Now that Will had shaped and coloured the thing, it came vividly to mental life. Jake, shaking his head, said, "Maybe I saw something."

Howard, joining them, said, "A snake won't strike unless you come at it. It was probably sleeping and you disturbed it." He was asserting mastery over the environment rather than looking into the claim. Will felt an illogical surge of liking for the man. "Check that it hasn't crawled into your clothes."

As they looked about, Will reached into his bag and, pretending to rummage, switched off the camera and turned it over. He pulled out his flannel and unwrapped it to reveal a soap dish. "It's only crappy hotel soap. I'll break it into three."

The paper wrapper said *Fenglin Hotel* in English under the Chinese. Will put that back in the bag, mindful that every trace of his presence was an incriminating spoor. He sliced the glassy white bar into three, and the men set to work, crouched in the shallows. It was not possible to work up much lather. The blood came off easiest where it had spattered skin that was already smeared with mud. It was most stubborn in Will's hair and under his fingernails. He rubbed until his skin was red and tingling, his cuts and scrapes stinging.

Jake said, "Maybe the snake should have bitten me."

"What do you mean?"

"Maybe it was meant to bite me. As punishment."

"It was just a dumb snake, and it's gone, so forget it."

"I have taken life," Jake said and the portentous phrasing made Will check Jake's expression to see if he was quite serious. Jake crouched, looking at his hands, red from rubbing. "There was a man and now he's dead. I did it and I can't undo it. I can't escape that. I feel bad."

"Don't be stupid. You'll feel better in a minute. Just get on with it, come on." Will put a hand on Jake's shoulder to jolly him along and fought back irritation – it was not yet time for reflection. Jake grabbed Will's hand with a fierceness that alarmed him, and squeezed it. Will didn't think he'd ever had a conversation with a naked man. It was awkward to look at him, so he sat and followed his gaze. The way sunlight sparkled on the surface of the water might, at another time, be endlessly engaging.

"I wish I hadn't. I just . . . I keep running it over in my head, and I wish it hadn't happened. Why? Why did it have to happen? Like that. Such a stupid thing. And it will never go away; it will be there every day, all the time. Right there, right in front of me. Every moment, every day. I think I want to die. What else can I do? There just isn't—"

"I can see . . . I can see how you could think like that. I can see how it is possible. But right now, this minute, you have a duty, a duty to yourself, to me, to carry on. And to him, too. Why should his death lead to another? Another total waste. Don't do that."

"I don't want to carry on."

"All right, look, we know this is a terrible thing. But it's past tense. It's a thing that happened."

Will would have liked to express his exasperation; maybe say it was all a bit late. But he was aware that the only thing to do was grind on. "You have to go forward from here. First of all, it wasn't your fault. The crossbow didn't work properly. That's probably why they were willing to sell it in the first place. That cop was killed by a faulty crossbow. Just as if you'd been driving a car and the brakes had failed and the car had hit someone. You weren't to blame. You were just unlucky. Mechanical failure. Hold on to that. Repeat those words."

"I feel so . . . There's nothing I can do about it. It's just there. And it will never go away."

Howard came over. "It's a dream. This time tomorrow it's all going to be over. You will have woken up. See all this? Imagine it's all in black and white. Like old TV. Then imagine that picture getting smaller and fuzzier, and then it's gone." He snapped his fingers. "Now stop talking shit and focus. You've brought a spare set of clothes?"

Jake nodded.

"So we have to ditch these bloody rags."

"We can throw them in the rubbish somewhere along the way," said Will.

"Have you not seen? There's people who go through garbage, looking for stuff they can sell. You want something scrutinised, put it in a Chinese garbage bin."

"What about leaving it in the forest?"

"Quality foreign labels with blood all over them? We have to sink them. You want to volunteer your bag for that task? It looks finished anyway; got holes all over it."

"Sure."

Jake and Howard stood around, naked and preoccupied, while Will emptied his bag. He didn't think there was anything in there to associate it with him, but he turned it inside out and shook it to make sure. Jake's friendship bracelet and necklace went into the back pockets of Will's shorts, which had a sturdy zip. Then everything went into Will's bag, and they filled it up with stones. It was good to have a task to focus attention on, and, finally, not such an unpleasant one.

Howard said, "I want to be sure it goes in as deep as possible. We'll take it out to the middle. Give me a hand, Will."

They swam it out into the lake awkwardly, each with a hand on a strap and the weight dragging them down and together. They had to kick hard to keep afloat, and at first, before they found a rhythm, they kept kicking each other. It was awkward, tiring work, and Will was about to suggest it was an unnecessary hassle, that Jake was right, they should have thrown the bag off the rock, when Howard spoke.

"He's all over the place. All that shit about killing himself."

This, then, was the real reason for the swim: a chance to have a quiet conversation.

"It's just talk. He's working it out in his mind. It's like you said. Soon as we get him out of here, he'll be fine," Will said.

Their faces were barely a foot apart. "You think he's going to hold it together? Now and for ever more? I don't know."

"He's having a comedown, too, remember? Who wouldn't be . . . showing the cracks?"

"Maybe he should kill himself. That would be ideal. Soon as he's the fuck away from me, he can go and slit his wrists, and that would be a weight off my mind, I tell you. He drinks, yes?"

"Sure."

"You can't trust a guy who drinks with a secret like this. Some day he'll get drunk and blab it all out. Could be next week, could be next year. I can't stay with the thought that everything is dependent on that fuckup keeping his big mouth shut. I don't want it hanging over me. Can't take that kind of risk."

Will was getting tired. He said, "Let's drop it."

"No, let's take it a bit further."

26

Will's arm was sore. He said, "I'm letting go," and opened his hand, and his body lifted as he kicked away. He launched himself backward and trod water, light now, balanced.

Howard dipped, then rose. He must have let go of the bag a moment later. He said, "What if Jake really was bitten by a snake and died? Or jumped off a cliff 'cause he couldn't take it any more. Or by accident tripped and fell off a cliff and broke his neck? We'd have to take his body back and say what happened, but, you know, there'd be two of us to say it. They'd have to believe us. And everything would be a bit more secure."

Will imagined the bag falling into darkness. He kicked back, gliding away, and looked back towards the shore. Jake stood with one hand on his hip. He looked a simple creature, just limbs, face, dick and hands. Will said, "If you kill Jake, I'm not backing up any bullshit story you make up. So you'll have to kill me as well."

"You're a brave man," said Howard. His upper body was still, but below the waterline pale blobs rippled: his legs as they pushed him on.

Going slowly backwards with big sweeps of his arms, Will said, "I'm just thinking it through. You can't kill Jake without me backing up your story. So, okay, I don't get onside – where does that leave you? You going to kill us both? I can't see it." He shook his head, and droplets spattered the water surface. "It would be tricky to arrange, for a start. Only one shot in that crossbow, after all. And even, say, you managed it you know it'll look suspect. You wouldn't be able to stroll out of here and say you lost two tourists. That's going to raise too many questions. It's even more risk to you than where you are now. I'm not brave. I'm relaxed. I'm very relaxed here. I'm heading back knowing that we're going to carry on with the plan we've decided on."

Howard said, "If he was more like you, I would have no worries at all." He turned away and struck out for the shore.

Will got out of the water and put on a clean T-shirt and shorts. The shorts had big pockets on the thighs, and everything else went in there: washbag, emergency kit, water bottle. The camera went round his neck.

Jake and Howard's fresh clothes were up in the Jeep. Naked but for shoes, they looked like a couple of earnest nudists. Will said, "I'm going first. I'm not looking up at your hairy arses." He was glad to turn his back on the lake and put one dusty foot in front of another in a trek away from it.

Howard said, "We need to get new shoes as soon as we can. These have got blood on, too."

Jake said, "You know those white pumps the peasants wear, with the red stripe? I want a pair of those."

"Warriors. They're good. Comfortable, and they're only twenty kuai."

"Stylish in an old-school way."

Will admired their attempt at conversation. He wanted to join in, to help construct the pastiche of normality, so he called back, "Considering your condition, you'd better mind these thorns."

"Trample them for us," Jake said. "Wouldn't want one of them swiping my dick."

"Yeah, that'd be a nasty accident."

Will regretted his words as soon as they were out, and he wished he could snatch them back. Hinting at the appalling events behind them, 'nasty accident' was exactly the wrong thing to say, and the ill-judged phrase seemed to hang in an awkward silence. It was scarely credible, he reflected, that even in this situation a person could care about saying the wrong thing. Jake would have known not to say it. Deciding to say nothing more, Will scrambled ahead.

He groped up a narrow, steep stretch of track between boulders. He felt he had been tramping up and down here for years, being batted by the same twigs, stubbing his toes on the same stones. He put a hand on a rock and pushed himself up, aware that for the next paces the path levelled and widened and could be taken quickly – and then he saw a snake coiled on a flat stone just ahead. He came to a nervous, stuttering halt.

The snake's head rose and swung towards him, radiating mild annoyance. It was striped black and green. The thing paused in what seemed deep consideration, tongue flickering though narrowly open jaws.

Will unbent and made himself still and said, "I don't want anything from you."

The snake uncurled and proceeded diagonally away, erasing itself, but it was Will who felt dismissed. He did not want to move forward, not for a few heartbeats, although he could see the path was clear.

"What did you say?" asked Jake.

"Nothing." The encounter was for him alone. Perhaps he had conjured the thing with his earlier cry, or perhaps it had come to rebuke him for his breakfast. It could mean whatever he wanted it to and as much or as little as he desired. Anyway, it was something to think about. He was glad it was gone but glad, too, to have met it.

Jake whispered, "Pick up the pace; I want to talk to you."

Will supposed Jake was going to have another go at defending his actions, and he did not look forward to whatever was coming. When Howard was six or seven paces behind, about where Will had seen the snake, he turned and said, "Well?"

Jake had a twig in his hand and used it to slash idly at clumps of foliage as he said, "I remember I had this T-shirt when I was a kid, said 'Shit Happens' on it. Really naff, obviously, but I thought it was daring. I never really thought about it. But it's true, isn't it? Shit happens. I'm going to get that tattooed. That is my new religion. The religion of shit happening." He threw the branch elegantly, with a javelin thrower's overhand. It flew straight, dipped, then splashed into the pool. The current caught it and bullied it into an eddy between boulders, where it spun fretfully. "I'm sorry about what I said earlier. I mean, about trying to give you money. That was a shitty thing to do. It put you in an impossible position. And I can see, looking at it with a bit of distance, that you were doing what you thought was right."

Will felt an unexpected surge of affection for his friend. Even after all of this, the pleasure he habitually derived from Jake's approval and affirmation was undiminished. Now, feeling the new and intriguing power that he had over Jake, he found it easy and pleasurable to exercise magnanimity. He said, "It's okay," and meant it.

"I didn't know what I was saying, I was just . . . you know, you say things in the heat of the moment."

"Forget it."

"I will make it up to you. Not with a new camera, mind, I'm not that generous." Jake shook his head, then abruptly quickened his pace. "So. What are you going to do when you get home?"

"I can't even . . . I don't know." Will shook his head, ostensibly to stir the entourage of wasps but as much to make the question go away. Even considering thinking about the future induced anxiety.

"I'm going to join an NGO," continued Jake. "I can start by volunteering for them over the summer holidays, then it won't be hard to get a job with them when I leave college."

"Do NGOs need lawyers?"

"'Course they do. And, if not, I'll dig wells for them. Answer phones. Whatever they need me to do." Jake grabbed a root with both hands and swung himself round a switchback. "I'm serious about that."

"It's a good plan."

"Isn't it? We have to live right. We're not bad people. This is a turning point. From now on, and forevermore,

I am going to do good. 'Cause that's what this has to lead to."

His voice had grown in volume, and something of the little speech must have reached Howard, for the man laughed sardonically as he shimmied round a spiky bush.

Jake glared at him, then reasserted his point as if being contradicted. "It has to lead to something good happening." There was an intensity to his gaze, as if he burned with a sudden religious conversion. It made Will uncomfortable. To neuter the atmosphere, he said, "I'm really thirsty."

"Will? I never copped off with Jess."

The abrupt change of subject caught Will unaware, and mental imbalance was reflected in his body: his foot skidded, knocking a pebble down the cliff. He watched it bounce away, kicking up puffs of dirt before being lost in the green. "It doesn't matter."

"I really didn't. I don't expect you to believe me, of course, but I'm telling the truth. Ask her about it when you get back. You're not going to be much inclined to believe her, either. But it is the truth."

Will resented the return of this particular trauma; as far he was concerned, it had been comprehensively superseded. "So why would you say you did?"

"'Cause I was sick of seeing you moping around after someone who – I'm sorry – just isn't into you. I wanted to do you a favour. I wanted you to get over it, move on. Honestly, I was quite angry that you didn't seem to want to." He shook his head in rueful recollection and tutted, then took big strides, leaving the matter and Will behind.

Will decided that it didn't matter, he didn't care, and it wasn't worth thinking about. He could hardly remember what it was like to be bothered by such trivialities, though he was aware that they had ruled his entire life up till today. None of his old problems existed any more. There was only one problem. He set his mind to it. It was all about destroying any evidence that might remain and getting out of the country as fast as possible. No need to wait till tomorrow and get the bus to Laos; as soon as they got back, he would find a ride to the border. He imagined himself being just another passenger on a nighttime highway, looking out of a grimy window at lights flickering past, and there was something so reassuring about the image of anonymity, rapid movement and darkness that he savoured it awhile. But gradually it brought another journey to mind, one that inspired only terror: they would soon have to trundle back along the track and past the customs checkpoint. And when he crested the clifftop and strode through the bush to the Jeep, that looked like a serious cause for concern.

For the Jeep seemed to scream murder. The mud spatters on the exterior had dried to a pale brown, which showed the bloodstains above the rear wheel and below the back door. The inside looked worse: dark puddles glistened on the floor, a thin slither pooled along the seam of the back seat, red smudges dotted the instrument panel and gearstick. The more Will looked, the more blood he saw. No surface seemed untainted.

Jake joined him and leaned in conspiratorially. "There's something in the boot, right?"

"Yeah."

"So let's ditch it." He wore a crafty, amused look. He could have been contemplating a practical joke. He was levelling out, something of his natural cheer returning. "Come on. He won't even notice."

"It's locked."

But Jake already had the driver's door open. He straightened and grinned and held up a toy robot, red with silver knees and elbows and big silver eyes. "He left these in the ignition." Keys tinkled on a ring at the end of a chain, attached to the top of the robot's helmet. "Let's show him we're not pushovers." Wearing a manic grin, Jake hurried to the boot. But the ignition key did not fit the lock, nor did the next key he tried, and there were at least five or six more.

"I don't want to make the situation any worse." Will fretted, shifting his weight from one foot to the other, and looked back towards the waterfall. Nothing of it could be seen through the thick foliage, the only clue to its presence the incessant roar and a freshness and sparkle to the air. When Howard arrived, they would receive no warning. Bushes would part, and he would appear as if through a stage curtain. It could happen at any moment. He had been only a few dozen paces behind.

"We'll dump it in the bush. He won't even notice till we're long gone," Jake said.

"This is a volatile situation, and we shouldn't be messing around."

"A last fuck-you."

"It's not worth it just to get one over on the guy."

Jake tried another key. "I don't want to travel anywhere in a Jeep full of contraband. Especially not after this. It's a rational decision."

Leaves rustled and Will winced in response, tensing up until he heard a receding pattern of disturbance and realised it was a bird flying away. Still, Howard must be almost upon them. He could picture the man taking big forward strides, eating up space.

At last a key slid in smoothly, the lock clicked and the lid yawned creakily, revealing a lumpy, bulging sack tied shut with red twine. It twitched.

Will flinched, banging his head against the lid.

"What the fuck?" whispered Jake.

27

Will looked again. The sack was still. He was in bright sunlight peering into darkness – perhaps it was a trick of the light. Or had he imagined it, given life to the inanimate, as he wished to do to that corpse?

Behind them, a rustling sound was getting louder. "He's coming," said Will, closing the boot, and it clicked back into place.

"There's someone in there," said Jake. "There's not much space. Has to be a kid. They steal boys and sell them. Remember?"

Only a couple of days ago, they had flicked through the English-language *China Daily*, a yellowing two-week-old edition found in the bookcase at a café: a couple surnamed Yen had had their little boy snatched from the side of the road. They had paid a private detective to find him, but no leads had been forthcoming. Hundreds of kids went missing in this fashion every year: couples desperate for an heir paid huge amounts for a boy.

Will's memory of the twitching sack was replaced by an image that was just as vivid, despite being imaginary: a child curled up, hot, delirious with panic, pale and shaking, a gag across his mouth, and his feet and hands tied.

"We could save a kid," said Jake.

"You want to take him on?"

"There's two of us."

"But—"

"Get your penknife out."

Will put his camera down and pulled the blade out on his Swiss army knife. It looked hopelessly puny, barely seeming to qualify as a weapon. Caveats sprang instantly to mind: It's small, I can't fight, I can't see how this is going to work out, I'm foggy, tired, and confused, all of which coalesced in the single plaintive idea that he did not want to be a hero, having neither the character, ability or inclination. He just wanted to go home. It was hard to care about the rather abstract problem of a kid he had not seen, still could not quite believe was there.

"It's just . . . it'll make . . . I can't think it through. We have to think it through."

Will's mouth was dry, and he felt queasy. It struck him as unfair that, after everything, there was this to go through. Was it possible to wear out an adrenal gland through over-use? It might at least learn to adjust to recent massively heightened stress levels and stop giving him such a hard time. It was a shame that mentally saying "Fuck it, fuck it, fuck it, I just don't care any more" was no help at all. Presumably, you had to truly believe it, rise above it like Buddha.

Jake snatched the knife. Howard approached, saying, "We'll stop by a pool or spring on the road back, clean up the Jeep. It'll be fine." His nakedness seemed strange and unexpected, a little obscene. Will noted how big his belly button was; the way the flesh wrinkling round it made it look like the pupil of a blind eye. "Those customs guys won't stop us. They'll barely even look at us, they'll remember us from before and wave us on. Believe me, I've done this before and you haven't; there is no cause for concern."

Jake heaved the sack out of the boot.

"What are you doing?" said Howard.

"Stay where you are," said Jake, waving the knife. "I'm letting the kid go. And you're not going to do anything about it."

"What are you talking about?"

Will coughed and shuffled. "I'm – I'm going to have to back him up on this."

Even as Jake sawed at the twine, Will realised their supposition was faulty. The sack was lumpy in the wrong way, the sporadic twitches and bulges seeming to indicate a set of shifting, independent forms rather than a person. When the twine was cut and the mouth of the sack opened, something like a snake flopped out and uncurled, and Will retreated till he noted the overlapping scales and the broad back and saw it as a tail. Pincering the lip of the sack between finger and thumb, he opened it wider and peered in at a glistening, iridescent blackness pricked with beady eyes and twitching snouts.

"Oh, what now?" said Jake. He upended the sack, and half a dozen squat creatures tumbled out. Each was about the size of a small dog, in body something like a fat, humpbacked lizard, but with the glossy overlapping scales of a dragon and the pointy long-nosed face. They looked like whimsical things of fantasy, half cute and half monstrous.

"What are they?" asked Will.

Howard said, "Pangolins."

Light seemed to bring them to life; they twitched and snuffled. But they couldn't move except to roll and thrash: they were trussed with twine, snouts tied shut, legs wrapped and pressed against the body.

Jake squatted, put a hand on a twitching creature to still it, and cut the twine that crossed its back. The trussing had been skilfully done with a single length – all the bonds began to unravel simultaneously and, in a frenzy of stubby limbs, the thing lashed and scrabbled free. A wobbly little torpedo, loosely packaged, it shot forward, bumped into Will's camera, retreated, turned, then flashed away.

Emboldened by his success, Jake turned a second creature onto its belly with his foot and straddled it. He pointed the penknife at Howard as he said, "Don't try to stop me."

Howard's response was to walk to the Jeep and pluck the keys out of the raised boot. In a show of studied unconcern, he turned his back and came over to settle with his hip against the side of the bonnet, one ankle crossed over the other, the pose of a man taking time out to enjoy the scenery.

Will breathed shakily out. After all, it seemed a new crisis had been averted. "You're not going to try and stop him. I think that's best."

The second pangolin loped away, trailing twine. It resembled a giant mechanical mouse and moved in as arbitrary a fashion. It circled the clearing, then shot into the bushes. "Go on, little critter," said Jake, and started on the next. Will admired his willingness to get right among the things, heedless of claws and teeth.

"Let him save a few animals," said Howard. "It can start rebalancing the cosmic order."

"How many of those things pays for the cop?" said Will. "Karmically speaking?"

"Would take a better philosopher than me to grapple with that one."

"What do you want them for?"

"The scales get used in medicine but, basically, they eat the things. They call it wild flavour."

"How much were you going to get for them?"

"I bought them for a thousand, and I can sell them on for three."

"Three thousand dollars?"

"Chinese yuan."

"That's what . . . two hundred quid profit? That's all this was ever about?"

28

The pettiness of the sum seemed to make it all worse. At least if the Jeep had been stuffed with, say, a million dollars' worth of heroin, high stakes would have made the murder of some consequence, less arbitrary and trivial. "I thought you were some big-time drug smuggler. You're so small-time. Restaurant smuggling. It hardly seems worth the risk. You must be desperate to do this, huh?"

"I wouldn't say desperate," said Howard.

"What would you say?"

"Inconvenienced. I entered a Mahjong game, it got out of hand, I ended up owing some money. Never should have got into it. I forgot a good rule: 'Know your game and stick to it.' You got a game?"

"I guess I'd have to say World of Warcraft," said Will.

"Him?"

"Call of Duty."

"I'm a Go man," said Howard.

"That's the one with black-and-white pieces?"

"Very simple. People play using stones and orange peel, the grid marked out with chalk on the pavement. Simple rules, too. But it's the subtlest game in the world. They've built a computer that can beat a man at chess, but there's no computer that can beat a Go master. Know why? Too many variations, too many moves; computational power is just not up there."

The last pangolin shot away. It was heading straight for Will. He hitched himself up onto the bonnet to get out of the way, and the thing barrelled into the front wheel and sprang back. It turned a frantic circle, then hauled itself swiftly into the Jeep, slipping under the front seat easily as a snake vanishing into a hole. Will got down and peered and saw eyes shining back and heard claws ticking on metal.

"He wants to come along," said Jake, giving Will his penknife.

"Open the door on the other side," said Howard, "and we'll scare him out."

Will sidled away. Let them deal with the critter. He looked forward to being out of their company. Howard was simple to think about: it was easy and uncomplicated to hate the man and never want to see him again. Jake was more of a problem. Will guessed that when they returned home he would want to excise Jake from his life and that the feeling would be mutual. And yet, what if they discovered – five or twenty years down the line – a restless need to talk about this? He wouldn't be able to discuss it even with a wife. Jake was the only person he could approach. This shared secret brought them together and divided them from the rest of humanity. Will considered the man – now bent over, shouting and making shooing gestures – and wondered whether he was looking at his new brother.

Jake stood, put his hands on his hips, and said, "The little fucker isn't shifting."

Howard twisted a branch off a tree.

"I'm not hitting it."

"Just poke it a bit. Go on. It'll get pissed off and hop out the other side."

"It's no use. Little fucker just hisses at me."

"Really lash it about. Come on. These things have hide like a coconut – you're not going to hurt it."

"You can do that if you want. Have you seen their claws?"

"Now it's really angry."

Will turned his back. He followed a kinking line of twine and found a pangolin crouched snuffling in the grass. The shield-shaped scales were largest at the top of its back; it looked like a walking pinecone. It glanced at him incuriously, and Will bent and put a hand out towards it, his fellow woodland sufferer, and nearly lost the end of his finger as the thing lashed out with a long curved claw. It bolted, dragging a frenetic streamer of twine, and Will retreated, feeling reproved. He had been incautious and only just got away with it. Everything here must be considered harmful until proved absolutely otherwise.

This was how it was to end, then: with a touch of ill-tempered farce. He looked about, feeling spurred to take the measure of this place, to sum it up, for momentous events had occurred here and he would never visit again. There was the track petering out, and stones and mud, and a hopeless conglomeration of leaves, with shafts of sunlight needling down through the canopy, picking out some for special attention.

He supposed he would never be able to think about pangolins or penknives, forests or Jeeps, China or crossbows, without being dropped back here, wincing at painful memories. He'd spend the rest of his days tiptoeing round mental trapdoors. No photographs would be needed to jog these memories. The one part of his trip he didn't want to document would be the one he could never forget.

He told himself not to be so morbid. Soon he would be far away in Laos, at Four Thousand Islands, lying in a hammock, mango smoothie in hand, tanned girls in bikinis reclining nearby, listening to birdsong and laughter, watching the sun set over the sluggish river, the sky streaked pink and red, the red bleeding out as the sun dipped, oozing like a knife wound. He dispelled the corrupted image by squeezing his eyes shut. But when he opened them, he saw real blood: rust-coloured flakes dotted his trainers. He would get new ones as soon as possible.

Thinking that engaging his companions would be preferable to any more disquieting introspection, he returned to the Jeep. Jake crouched beside the open driver's door, aiming Will's camera.

"Hey," called Will. "Leave that alone."

"It still isn't shifting. I thought the flash might scare it out." Jake started pressing buttons. "How do you . . . ah, got it."

The camera flashed, and the response was immediate: the pangolin flew from under the front passenger seat and barrelled straight at Jake, who stepped back, stumbled and fell on his arse. The pangolin zipped once round the clearing, came back to the Jeep, and dived straight back under the seat.

Jake smiled and Howard chuckled. They looked at each other and laughed, then laughed at being able to laugh.

But it was only a flicker. The fragile levity broke and a cloud dropped when Howard said, "Did you take a picture? We can't have any pictures."

"I don't think so. I'll check."

Will was smiling wanly as he hurried over, hands out. "Let me, please. Give it to me. I'll do it."

But Jake was already pressing buttons. He said, "What's this?" frowning at the display screen.

29

A tingling heat rushed into Will's cheeks. He had an idea that the situation could be saved if he got the thing back quickly. So he accelerated, but Jake retreated faster, and when Will heard the tinny hiss of the audio he faltered, realising that urgency on his part would be immediately suspicious and might condemn him. He had to appear nonchalant and hope that Jake did not understand what he had chanced upon. After all, the screen was barely five centimetres square and not easy to see in direct sunlight. The incriminating film would be upside down, jerkily shot, and mostly out of focus. Anyway, most of the footage would be images of leaves and sky. Ordering himself to stay calm, Will held out a slow hand. "Give me my camera back."

Heavy breathing and metallic clunking became audible over the crackles and rustles.

Jake was frowning, shading the screen with a cupped hand. "This looks like the path down to the waterfall. I recognise that creeper."

Will said lightly, "Sometimes it bumps and switches on." He glanced aside at shaggy green. He could strike out off the track and thrash in hard, and maybe he'd have enough of a head start to lose them quickly. But the lush

wildness intimidated him, and things were not desperate yet. He reached out and, trying to sound casual, said,
"Hard drive's full of that kind of random crap."

"What's that? It looks like handlebars. Is that the bike?
That's the bike. That's the cop's bike."

"Show me," said Howard.

Jake hurled the camera over Will's head. Will swivelled
to follow it. It span as it arced up, then seemed to falter
and, with the lens aimed at the sky, dropped. Howard's
hands came together on it and pulled it down and to him.
Will realised his mouth was hanging open. He shut it. He
snapped, "Stop throwing that around. What do you think
you're doing?"

Howard's voice swelled scratchily out of the fuzz of
bad audio, saying, "We need to get him tied to the bike.
It'll hold him down." It went on, excruciatingly, into a
shocked and ringing silence, devoid even of the hum of
insects: "We'll throw him off the overhang."

"Fucker filmed the whole thing," said Jake.

Howard shaded the screen. "There's the body, the bike,
and us chucking him into the water."

Jake said, "It must have been hidden in his bag."

"Insurance in case things went wrong," said Will
quickly. "You two said you'd club together and pretend
I did it, remember. You were quite open about that as a
possibility. I wanted a record. Just in case."

Howard was shaking his head. "This is a serious abuse
of trust. Fuck, man, you got an admission of murder on
film." He raised the camera in one hand and shook it.
"This is bullets in the back of the head."

"Hey," said Jake, "you know when he said there was a

snake? That was to stop me looking in the bag, where he'd hidden the camera. There was no snake."

"Although, in another way," said Howard, "there was a snake after all."

"I'll delete it," said Will, and stepped towards Howard. "Give me the camera, and I'll do it. Come on. I'll wipe the film."

"A bit of editing, and you could have taken yourself off it. I think you were planning blackmail."

"Self-defence. You shouldn't have said you'd blame it on me. Just delete the film and we'll carry on."

Howard swung the camera at him. Will leaned away, but the edge caught him on the side of the head. He stumbled, dizzy and fogged, then Howard jabbed the lens in his face. Lashed with pain, Will went down on his knees, hands on his head. Howard loomed, dark and flat against the sparkling greens above.

An expanding black blot was the camera coming down. Will ducked, and displaced air moved over his face, the nearest thing to a breeze he'd felt in a while. He scrambled backwards, digging in his heels and rasping along on his behind, then flipped over, put his head down and scrambled into the brush. His centre of gravity was hopelessly forward, and for seconds he seemed poised on the verge of plunging face first into the ground, but by taking big steps and windmilling his arms he brought himself upright, and his scramble grew into the poise of a run. But he was only heading hard into green darkness, and the plants thickened treacherously. Lashing branches seemed another expression of Howard's anger. Heavy leaves slapped wetly at Will's legs. He felt he was flailing slowly through a thickening green medium and making a tremendous noise, a crackling like fire.

His one thought as he blundered was escape; he was as dumb and concentrated as the pig he had seen. Only he did not have that creature's density, and he could not force his way through. The forest pulled his legs away. He fell into a mass of thick-edged serrated leaves and, trying to escape, he only thrashed himself deeper in, so he hung suspended, drowning in the stuff. He wriggled backwards to get out and felt a hand on his leg. He was too late. Howard leaned over him. He slapped Will's cheek, then coarse fingers went around his neck. The skull ring dug in. Will spasmed in complaint but only sank deeper, with a sound like tearing sheets. Twigs jabbed into his back. Howard's hot hand squeezed, and he leaned in close, and Will felt the man's warm damp breath on his face.

Howard held the camera and, distractingly, the film still played on the little screen. Will heard his younger, stupider self say, "Did you really have to kill him?" and Howard replying, "It had to be done."

The real Howard said, "Nice one. Wish I'd thought of it." He let go of Will's neck and leaned back.

30

"How do you get into this?" said Howard. "I haven't got the fingernails for it. Ah, I got it." He prised open the camera's SD slot and popped out the memory card.

On the film, the body slid into the water.

Howard said, "How come it's still playing?"

Will rubbed his neck. "It's running from the internal memory."

"It's stored on here, too, right?"

"Yes."

"Excellent." Howard took out his keys. He popped off the toy robot's head, slid the memory card inside, and put the head back on. "You ever play Go?"

"No."

"You should learn."

"I'll think about it."

"Don't play against me. I'm good."

"I believe it."

"If you mention that I took this memory card, I'll deny it. And I'd say Jake is in no mood to believe you. Together we'll smash your camera and who knows what else. But just stay quiet, go with the flow, and nothing will happen. I'll even let you keep the camera."

He tapped Will's cheek. "Me and you, we're a couple of bums. But we've got clear heads. We know how it is. College boy out there, he don't. He's not like us. And he's got a lot to lose. You know what I'm saying?"

"I don't see how that film can be used to blackmail him. It incriminates all of us."

"The point is, it incriminates him. Stop thinking in this either/or way. Start thinking like a Go player. It's all about possibilities, shades of grey, manoeuvrings, the big what-ifs." He stepped back and pulled at Will's T-shirt. "Come on, let's get you out of there." Twigs snapped and cracked as Will came out. The jabbing in his back went away and left him merely sore. He stood woozily and rubbed his neck.

"You all right?" said Howard. "Make it look convincing. Act like I've been really beating up on you."

"You have."

"No, man – if I'd beat up on you, you wouldn't be talking. So what college your friend going to?"

"Why don't you ask him?"

"I might just."

"Where in Canada are you from?"

"Maybe I'm not from Canada at all."

Will was dazed and bruised and covered with leaves and twigs. He didn't think he needed to pretend anything. Howard grabbed his ripped T-shirt and escorted him back through the forest, and they crashed back onto the track, coming out close to the canyon edge. Howard waited till he heard Jake head towards them, then he spun Will, threw him down, and said, while making threatening gestures with the camera, "Dirty fucking weasel, I should kill you, you dirty fucking weasel, smack you to bits with your own camera. It's what you deserve."

Jake got in front of Howard, hands out, palms forward, his feet planted wide, saying, "All right, leave it. Leave it, that's enough. Enough. All right. Enough. Will, are you all right?"

"Yeah."

"Howard, he's learned his lesson. We'll leave it there." He helped Will up. "I'm disappointed, Will, disappointed and angry. We have to trust each other or this whole thing is going to blow up in our faces." He delivered his statement as if from a lectern; he had obviously been preparing it. "We have to act on a solid foundation of trust, but if you're going to break that foundation, we can't build on it."

Will felt he would rather be down in the mud for a while longer, to delay the moment when he looked Jake in the eyes. The words were ready; he would only have to whisper them – 'Howard took the SD card, I think he's going to try to blackmail you' – but they seemed heedlessly risky, a sure route to even more uncertainty and conflict, and it was so much easier to go with the flow and say nothing and, after all, a strong argument could be made that he owed Jake no favours. He faltered and opened his mouth to speak, then Jake said, "We're going to have to break your camera," and made it easy for him. Will clamped shut.

Howard shook his head. "It's been a long day, and we've all done some rash things. Let's just delete the film and pretend it never happened. He won't try and play tricks like that again, will you?"

"No."

"There you go. So you get your camera."

"But—" said Jake.

"When we're back. I'm keeping it till then. That good for you, Jake?"

"Okay. But delete the film right now."

"Absolutely. So you press this button here? Jake, come and watch. It's important that we all see what's going on." They craned over the glowing screen. "Look at this, like the three musketeers."

The film was playing, shot from a static position now. The camera was on the beach.

The focal point was the waterfall, on the right side of the frame, and the prickle of spray and the shine on wet rock were crisply captured. The lake was a fuzzy band of darkness shot through with pale streaks and blobs and interrupted on the left side by the image's most striking verticals – three fuzzily pink naked figures standing waist-high in the water. Their features were not distinguishable, but it was possible to tell them by frame and posture: Will the palest and tubbiest, Howard the thinnest and darkest, Jake the most pleasingly proportioned. The hazy figures cavorted in spatters of light, and there was nothing to indicate they weren't having a laugh in an arcadian idyll.

"Good shot of your lily-white arse, there, Jake," said Howard.

"Just delete it," said Jake as, on the soundtrack, his simulacrum shouted, "Haven't you got some soap?" and started to slough out of the water. The tiny Will figure put his hands on his head and ran them through his hair. Oh yes,

Will knew what was coming next – he was about to shout, 'Snake!' Reliving the moment, he twitched with panic.

"This button here?" said Howard. "Everyone gather in very close to see it being pressed. That's right, real close, heads touching."

"Shit," said Jake, the real one. "What's that?"

"Your arse," said Howard.

"No, there, behind the waterfall. That shape there."

"It's a rock or something."

"I saw it move."

"I'm going to delete it."

"No stop," snapped Jake. "Freeze the film. Freeze it."

"All right. Happy?"

"Now rewind a bit. I'll do it."

"No, you show me which button to press, and I'll do it."

"Not too far. It was about there. There. Now, stop and play."

"I don't see what the big deal could be," said Howard. "It's just rocks."

They watched, eager and unblinking, the tiny screen seeming to suck them in, jewel-like and intricate, a whole other world.

"How can it be a rock if it moves? Play it again from there, and watch the background. There."

A pale shape behind the waterfall uncurled, grew bent limbs, and came crouching forward. It seemed fleeting and ambiguous, as likely to dissipate back into water as to continue, and that gave it the look of something magical, a manifestation or special effect.

"It could be a trick of the light." Will said it because he wanted it to be true, but any possibility of doubt soon vanished. A slim figure was coming from behind the waterfall: a head, shaded by a raised hand, interrupted the curtain of spray, causing momentary sputters. It was a girl, Will was sure by the slim limbs, and she was looking to see if the coast was clear. It wasn't. She hurriedly retreated, folding back into glossy darkness.

"Oh, shit," said Howard.

Jake said, "There's someone down there," and squeezed his lower lip between finger and thumb.

Howard nodded slowly, rubbing his chin. "Yeah."

31

Their gazes locked, moved uneasily away, returned. Will looked down at the camera display. The film played on and now showed Jake standing with his feet together, scanning the ground. Will stopped it, rewound, and found the place again. There was no mistake – there she was again, a little, long-limbed creature, and it was as shocking as the first time.

Will mentally rewound the real event and tried to see it from her perspective.

She would have watched the men zigzag down the path with their burdens. Perhaps she had been on the verge of calling out to them but had been stilled by their solemn demeanour. Then she would have watched the body tumble and break, and started to fear. And there was no retreat. She could do nothing but stay quiet behind the sheet of water, which was nowhere near cover enough, and hope the men were too engrossed to spot her.

Will paused the film and deleted it, but it was not easy to break away from the reassuringly two-dimensional problem, so easily solved with the press of a button, and for some seconds more he looked down at the screen, reflecting their three troubled heads. Each had stubble, dark rings under the eyes and a furrowed brow. It made them look so familiar, you would have thought they were brothers.

Howard was the first to rise. He trudged to the clifftop and looked down. "Must be there." He pointed at the waterfall.

"Who could it be?" said Jake.

"I don't know. Shit, man, this is unlucky. This is very unlucky. We're in the middle of nowhere. No one should be here." He threw up his hands, as if complaining to the malicious god who was toying with him, and repeated, "No one should be here." The hands came down and straightened his bandana. "Could be a refugee from Burma, maybe. Ran over the border, got lost. Though why someone would head down there, I don't know. The path is an obvious dead end."

"There could be more than one," said Jake.

Will said, "I know who it is." He did not want to look at his companions, so he fixed his gaze on swirling water. He was aware of them scrutinising him but not of their expressions. "It's the girl, my girl. What's her name, I can't remember her name. I left some money down there."

After he had forced those words out, the rest escaped in a rush. "Right there, right where she is. I put it in a crack in the rock. The two of them must have gone in there together. I guess she noticed it, but if she picked it up in front of her friend she'd have to share it. So she came back on her own after the other girl left. To pick up the money."

"Must have got here just before us," said Jake. "What were you leaving money for?"

"I felt sorry for them. I wish I could remember her name."

Jake was saying, "This is . . ." He struggled for words, and Will wondered if he would come up with something useful, but all he could finally get out was "fucked up". He put his hands flat on his cheeks and dragged them down. His little fingers pulled his glistening lower lip over, his mouth forming a fishy pout.

"The problem with charity", said Howard, as if lecturing in a classroom, "is it always has these unintended consequences." His voice was brusque, even chirpy, and when he turned and headed to the Jeep it seemed for a moment that he intended them to carry on as before – just get in and drive away. It was what they all wanted, after all.

That comfortable illusion faded when Howard returned with the crossbow.

"Wait," said Will. "Howard, you said those girls were refugees, right? Owned by nasty people, people you're scared of. They'll be afraid of them, too. So she'll know not to say anything. She won't talk."

"Oh yeah, I remember. 'Fucking truckers for a bowl of rice.' No, sorry. That was all bullshit. I said that to keep you quiet. They're a couple of village girls." He hefted the crossbow over his shoulder. In his other hand, he held the quarrels. "They're from that village we stopped in, remember it? They got trails – you can walk here faster than we drove."

"They won't talk," said Will. "They'll know not to talk. We don't have to do anything, let's go. Come on, let's just leave. Please. Nothing changes, let's go."

He had a sense of the situation rushing away from him and words being things that could stake it in place. But as soon as the words were out, they seemed thin and powerless. It was no good – his own voice annoyed him, it was a hectoring bleat – so he stopped talking, shutting his mouth with an audible plop.

He went to the cliff edge. The waterfall was endlessly varied yet always the same. He imagined a speck in that uselessly beautiful cascade – imagined it rushing down, spinning round the pool, turning in a lazy arc round the rocks before picking up speed as the current caught it and forced it bumping along the rapids. That was how he felt, swept along, and he wanted to resist.

The distant pool looked hard as glass. He told himself it was too late to stop, even if he wanted to. Before the instruction was quite conscious, he took another step and jumped.

Blues and greens swirled in a sunlit interval, and he reflected that this fall was going on longer than any he had ever felt before, so long that it had time to become a thing in itself, a state of being. Sick foreboding spread from a core in his stomach, and he tensed against it before water crashed into him. It seemed to wall him in; and a new kind of descent began, darker and more frightening, then he was inside something he recognised, the tug of a current. He slowed into what seemed a cold dark room and thrashed towards the palest corner. As he approached the surface, he saw sunlight shimmer and splinter, and he reached for it and was spat out of that smothering hug into light and air. He opened his mouth wide and sucked the whole scene.

Will was pained in new ways, but once he circled his limbs in the water he knew none of it was bad. He bobbed,

coughing and spluttering, enjoying the feeling of buoy-
ancy, which seemed a sign of triumph, like being carried
aloft by a crowd. He realised that the slow clapping he
could hear was not part of him, unlike the blood pounding in his head and the rasp of breath, but was coming
from above. His gaze moved up the cliff, and he noted
how forbidding it appeared, a fortification of rock and
roots. How far he had come, and how fast.

At the crisp edge where earth stopped and sky began,
two figures stood dark and flat as shadow puppets. Jake
was shading his eyes with both hands. Howard was
applauding, so slowly that there was time to hear the echo
of each clap die before the next came. He called, "And
how is this going to help?"

Will turned away and struck out for the waterfall, feeling himself a big, blundering animal. The torrent fell in
rippling sheets and lashing ropes and buzzed like static.
As he got closer, he saw a human form, dim and indistinct, flicker eerily in the glassy darkness behind.

She squatted with her knees pressed together, shoulders hunched, hands tight on her calves. Her soaked black
tunic clung to her skin. Her head rose as he approached,
and when Will passed through the sheet of water into
her misty private space she unfurled and stood with her
feet wide apart, eyes narrowed, pressed back against the
rock. She was pointing a knife. Drawn into herself, she
reminded him of the snake he had met on the boulder,
swaying behind a force field.

She shivered, with cold or fear, presumably, and the
blade trembled. Her hair was plastered to her face and
neck. The skin under her nose and eyes was red and puffy.

Perhaps she had been crying, or maybe it was an effect of the water; she had been here a long time.

Will spread his hands. "Look? No weapon. Nothing." He took a small step forward. Pointing up, he said, "They will try to kill you. Run away. Do you understand? Run away. You have to go."

The knife, the spray and the din of the water were all distracting. Blundering on, Will felt irritated and foolish, aware of being an absurd figure – the archetypal tourist trying to make the locals understand by shouting at them. "Don't . . . You don't need to point that at me. You need to run away."

He mimed running but without moving his legs, as he didn't want to lose his footing. He jiggled his knees and waist and pumped his arms in what he supposed must look like a clumsy dance. "Run away. They've got a crossbow." This mime was easy – he sketched an imaginary one, hefted it, aimed and pulled the trigger. She seemed to understand that, as it instigated a bout of wailing. It was dispiriting to see her lower lip quiver and hear that noise from deep in her throat. Her knuckles whitened on the knife handle.

32

Outside, Howard was shouting, the words rising scratchy and indistinct above the water and the bawling of the girl. "Will, I don't know what you think is happening here. We should put a lid on the paranoia and relax for a second. Will, come on. Come out of there, come out, and we'll make a plan."

The girl hunched with the knife protruding in front of her face like a tongue. Of course, as far as she was concerned, Howard could be telling Will to hurry up and get on with murdering her. Though she was only half his size, she seemed twice as concentrated, and Will supposed they were an even match.

"You've got no chance in here. Get out there." He ducked, hands over his head, mimicking how he wanted her to flee. "Stay low, and I don't think they've got a shot. Please, just go. You've got time, but you have to go now. Now."

To get out, she would have to pass him, so he pressed against the curving rock wall to give her space. He slipped, lost his footing and slid, landing with a bump on his arse. He was no threat – that could not be clearer, could it? A more bumbling, foolish figure could hardly be imagined.

Her route to the outside was clear – just three or four easy steps. It was her only sensible course of action, surely. Yet she remained obdurately poised behind the quivering blade.

"Oh, just get out," Will snapped.

He realised he disliked her. All he knew about her was that she had a good line in false smiles. The only time he had seen her exercise free will was to try and cheat her friend out of a share in a hundred-yuan note. Furthermore, she didn't seem too bright, was mistrustful and had a tendency to jump to erroneous conclusions.

She took a step forward.

"Yes, that's right."

The girl lunged at him, jabbing with the knife. The blade was small, with a blunt point but a decent edge. Will flinched and blocked it with an open hand and felt it tremble in the handle. His palm stung, and warmth spread down his wrist. He was bleeding from a shallow cut at the base of his thumb. It wasn't deep, but it was shocking to see his own blood. He had seen a lot today, but little had been his. He felt frustrated and annoyed more than hurt.

"Idiot," he yelled, shaking his stinging hand. Blood spattered the rock. "I'm trying to help you." Exasperation seemed to work where explanation and entreaty hadn't: she edged her way round to the mouth of the cave and peered out.

Will scrambled to the opposite side of the cave entrance. Water pounded his head and streamed down his neck. He cupped his hands over his eyes. He was looking not through a single sheet of water but several, all of different widths, arranged in a complicated and changing array.

CHAPTER 32

It was like gazing through shifting lenses. He located Howard's bandana, a vivid dash of red in a guttering blur of green and grey. The man was standing near the bottom of the path with his hands on his hips. Will couldn't see the crossbow, but perhaps it was on the ground, ready to be snatched up.

The girl could come out of the cave and turn a hard right and splash along the cliff face to the big rocks and shallow water on the far side of the pool. Then she could hurry across a narrow pebble beach and into the safety of the thick foliage on the riverbank. Once she was in there, she would be lost in the green and only had to hurry downstream.

He pointed out the route and made encouraging motions. "Go. Go, run. As soon as you get across the pool, you're fine. You just have to get across the pool."

It would be a nervous run, especially the first part. She did not have to swim – she could wade through the shallows and hop from rock to rock – but there was no cover. Howard would have one shot, for sure. Will realised that he might as well be collaborating with the man, given the task of flushing her out. Yes, the way things were working out, that interpretation fitted the facts as much as any other. Well, it was her own faul; she should have left when he arrived. At least he was trying. He felt sorely unappreciated.

Howard was shouting again. "Will, you have to come out now. We all appreciate your efforts, we're impressed, but let's move on together on this."

The girl ran out of the cave. Will had no idea why she chose that moment: the fact that he was distracted, or something about Howard's tone, or maybe some tipping point of courage or desperation had been reached. The torrent spurted and hissed as she passed through it, and in a moment she was gone.

Will stayed right where he was. There didn't seem any point in following her, though he was uneasily aware that once again he had retreated to the useless role of witness. The bullying thump of the water on his head could have been a rebuke.

Through flickering translucent sheets, he watched Howard bend and pick up the crossbow, then go down on one knee and settle it into his shoulder. Will could see only the broadest movements. It could have been a jerky animation of a stick figure, but his imagination completed the picture: the straining wood, the taut string, the quarrel's point. He remembered the man's earlier words with reference to the cop – "make it pop like a watermelon."

He looked towards the figure of girl, but found he was able to consider her only through the corner of an eye. He was braced and wincing like a passenger who could see the coming crash and could do nothing about it. She was in the shallows, close to the beach, and skittered from rock to rock, trying to keep her balance with skinny outstretched arms. She looked small, pathetic and precious. She slipped and cried out, then Will heard a clatter, and in a narrow interval where a strip of the cascade of water was clear as a window he glimpsed a rod, conjured out of nothing, snapping against a stone. The pieces twirled away and landed in the water.

33

The event did not fufil Will's expectations of what real, lethal acts of violence looked like. It was rather undramatic. Disappointingly so, in a way – such momentous acts ought to be marked by decent noise and effects. Without them, it didn't feel quite true, and he had to reinforce the event with words: Howard had shot at the girl. Though Will hadn't seen the bolt until it had broken on the rock, and he hadn't heard it at all, when reimagining it he saw the quarrel as an airy blur and heard it whoosh.

Howard had shot at her. In a way, Will felt satisfied: he was vindicated, he wasn't wrong, the situation was as desperate as he'd thought, he hadn't foolishly misread anyone's intentions. Still, it was shocking to see it. Howard didn't just want this girl dead; he wanted to actively kill her, to shoot her with a crossbow and then come and finish her off, with a knife or with hands on her neck, while she cried with pain. It seemed scarcely credible. How astonishing for someone to want to kill someone else. He almost admired the strength of will that such a ruthless act required. It was a kind of decisiveness he felt he could not hope to achieve.

The girl got up, shrieked and turned round on the spot. The safety of the green was a long way off. Stumbling, waving her arms, she splashed right back towards the waterfall. She burst through it and scuttled past him and came to rest against the back of the cave, making a high keening sound from the back of her throat.

Will groaned. "You could have made it; he wouldn't have been able to reload in time. You should have kept going. Why didn't you keep going?"

Then he saw the blood on her stomach between the tunic and the skirt, and concern replaced anger. A splinter of the broken crossbow bolt must have flown up and slashed her. She held a hand over her wound and hopped from one foot to the other. She was looking at Will, frowning, lips pursed, as if this were all his fault and he should make amends.

Howard was swimming towards them, a slow head-high breaststroke. "Oh Christ, oh fuck," said Will. Was what he thought really happening? It seemed incredible. A murderer should not approach at such a ponderous pace. It was so hard to know what to do, and he felt in danger of slipping into a fatalistic inertia. He talked to spur himself into action. "He's coming to kill you. What am I supposed to do? What should I do?"

He took out his Swiss army knife. It looked piteously earnest and innocent, and even with the blade unfolded it seemed trivial, a cute facsimile of a proper weapon. How should a knife be held? With the blade pointed up or down, in one hand or two? It was good to have these practical concerns; they reassured him that he knew what he was doing. If only the blade would stop shaking. Even gripping it harder didn't steady it. The quiver was coming from his core, and he told himself it was because of the cold.

He watched Howard rise and stand on a rock just outside the cave, up to his knees in swirling water, and realised that he had joined the girl in making noises in his throat. He swallowed fear back with a gulp.

Will shouted, "I've got a knife." He had stepped onto this path without considering where it would lead. No doubt, in Howard's eyes, he had proved sentimental, unreliable, unable to ride the dark horse. Probably the man would want to kill him as well as the girl, simply to be safer in the future. And he had put himself in this terrible position out of what – altruism? No. Morality? Not really. It was just squeamishness, shame. But mostly guilt, because it was all his fault. If he hadn't left the money, she wouldn't have returned, and if he hadn't filmed the body's disposal, she wouldn't have been discovered. As the figure responsible for endangering her life, sadly, exasperatingly, he had the responsibility to try and preserve it.

Howard's slim, tanned form loomed on the other side of the stuttering gush of water. "Will, we understand. We're impressed. But you haven't thought it through. She saw the whole thing, she knows who we are. I know it's a shitty thing to be contemplating, and I'm not proud of it. But if she lives, we die."

"No more killing."

"Killing is what is going to happen to us if we get caught. And, you know, I don't think two's so different. From killing no one to killing someone, that's a big jump to make. From killing one to killing two, I'd say not so much."

Will's heart was beating fast. He was breathing heavily, and there was a sickly tightness in his stomach. Trying to keep his anguish out of his voice, he repeated, "I've got a knife."

"There's no need for any threats. Let's none of us do anything rash. Come out and we'll discuss it."

"No."

"This situation is new to all of us. We're all struggling to deal with it, and you've gone with your first, unconsidered response. I'm hoping you'll take a sober look at your present position and realise that it is . . . uncontinuable. Don't worry. I want to reassure you that you can turn off this road at any point, and there will be no comeback. I'm willing to overlook it," said Howard, "and I'm confident we can put it behind us. But you will have to come out. You will have to do that."

The girl's hand landed on Will's shoulder. She was crouching right behind him. His role was no longer ambiguous: she had accepted him as her protector, and that gave him strength. "I can't let you do it. I'm not coming out. If you come in here, I'll stab you."

"It's a horrible feeling to stab someone. You have to put a lot of effort into it, really force the knife in, twist it, pull it out, do it again – you're kind of digging a hole. It's a terrible thing, will give you nightmares your whole life. That what you want to do? You want to do that?"

"If I have to."

Howard tutted. "Be a bit more bamboo about this, Will. Come on, bend with the wind. Stubborn maintenance of a position can be admirable, but flexibility is an important asset. You're just . . . This is not helping. All right, fuck it, you know, I could go back and get that crossbow, and fuck it, fire the thing in there, see what I hit. Take out an arm or get lucky and bag me a gut shot. Yours or hers, who can say, I'm not going to fucking care. I don't want it to come to that, but it is on the table. That's going to be a grisly way to go, shot in a fucking dark, wet cave."

"There's a bend in the rock here. We can hide." Will glanced back. Theoretically, yes, if they arranged themselves tightly at the back of the space, they would be partially covered by a turn in the rock. The prospect, though – crouching, wincing, waiting to be shot at – was terrifying.

"Will, this is us. It isn't anything else. It's where we are. You know, if you get in my way, what will happen. If I have to come in and get the both of you, that's what I'll do."

Will reminded himself that his opponent was a skinny middle-aged guy. Probably with no more idea about knife fighting than he had. Howard would be coming at him through the torrent; he would be pounded by it, blinded, too, and struggling to find a footing on slippery rock.

Whereas Will was braced and steady; all he had to do was lunge. He practised, lashing his knife arm out, careful not to overextend and lose his balance. It could not be so hard to stab another person. If you didn't think about what you were doing and just did it, made the arm perform this simple mechanical motion, it was surely pretty easy. The trick, clearly, was not to think about it. Just do it, do it, do it, he chanted in his head, aware of but suppressing other voices, of fear and revulsion. Coiling into himself, he waited, feeling light but steady.

Water dribbled down his face, streams running on either side of his nose, then over his lips. He had to keep blinking and wiping his eyes. But his mouth felt dry and chalky.

Howard said, "You'll have to come out of there eventually."

Something hit him hard from behind, and he overbalanced, lurching forward. He skidded and fell forward into the torrent, which hit him like a door slamming down. He sprawled onto rock and glimpsed Howard, a metre or so away, stepping away backwards. Then Will rolled into churning water. Currents snatched, and cold lances spiked into his mouth and ears. He groped and thrashed and came up into brightness, sucking air and coughing.

34

The girl was groping her way along the rocks at the side of the cliff. Howard was wading after her, bringing his knees up high and pumping his arms to move faster through the water.

The knife in Howard's fist glittered. Will had lost his. He realised what had happened: she had shoved him out, using him as a diversion. It was only luck that he hadn't been injured on the rocks, impaled on his own blade, or stabbed by Howard.

And she had bought herself only a few seconds. She was six or seven paces in front of Howard.

What could be done? Will was nothing but an appalled spectator. He watched the girl step from shallow water onto a boulder, then skip across the rocks. Howard followed. With their waggling arms and varied steps, there was something of a dance about the wobbly chase. It even seemed that their bodies were rhyming: when the girl lurched left, Howard was lurching right, and when the girl landed on a boulder on hands and knees, Howard was jumping from another.

To a stranger, it would have looked like a game of kiss-chase in a bucolic idyll. Only Howard's knife and the blood streaking the girl would sabotage the interpretation, but they could seem like minor details in such a grand and pleasing arrangement of rock and twinkling water.

Howard took a big step, lost his footing and cried out as he slipped. The girl reached the surer ground of the pebble beach and sprinted for the treeline. In moments she was gone, the only sign that she had ever been there a flickering among the leaves.

When they were still and she was thoroughly erased, Will looked at Howard. The man lay beached, half in the water, half on smooth rock, propped up on one elbow, one hand gripping his ankle. His lips were pinned back, revealing gritted yellow teeth.

Will splashed unhurriedly towards him. "What's wrong?"

"Broke my fucking ankle. Help me out here, come on."

"You really think?"

"I'm not going to do anything to you now, am I? The girl's gone. We just have to hope she doesn't talk. Come on, help me up here."

"Drop the knife."

"All right. Here. See?" Howard flung his blade bad-temperedly into deeper water, and it vanished with a plop. Will helped him to his feet, and Howard put an arm around his neck, and they hobbled round the side of the pool.

"You be okay to drive?" Will asked.

"I'll have to be."

"I don't think she'll talk."

"Maybe. But maybe not. Probably not. We better hope not."

All passion was gone; they could have been fishermen giving up after a long fruitless day. There were only fading disgust and a vague disappointment. What a hassle all that had been.

But the girl was alive. Everything else, Will was sure, would work out, too, somehow.

"Where's Jake?" Howard asked.

"Up with the Jeep."

"You know what?" said Howard. "I really don't think she'll talk to the police." They were crossing the bubbling rapids, stepping awkwardly across stones and shallow water, towards the little beach. "There's nothing in it for her. She'd only be making people angry, stirring up trouble, and she'd know that. She's not stupid, that one, she's shrewd. She's got focus, ambition. Wants to raise a stake, go to the city, and get a job as a dancing girl. You know they got those ethnic dancing shows all over, for the Chinese tourists. Shake that long hair about, jangle some jewellery. Always combing her hair or practising her moves, though it don't look much more sophisticated to me than head-banging, I have to say. No, talking about this, about what she saw, it won't help her get where she wants to go. It's not shrewd." He looked into the dense forest on the riverbank. "You know what the shrewd move would be? Blackmail. She's got me by the balls – she'd work that out. 'Get me a comb made of bone, Mister. A dozen combs. A generator and a TV. My cousin needs his motorbike repaired.' Shit."

"I think she'll leave it. She won't do anything. You frighten her."

"I can't take the risk. I guess I can't stay around, not with that . . . possibility hanging over me. However faint.

I'll just . . . I'll go away. Well, I'd had enough of this place anyway. I could go . . . Lots of places I could go. Maybe I'll quit Asia altogether. Check out Africa."

"I keep hearing talk about Madagascar."

"That so?"

"Madagascar is the new place, apparently. Beaches, nice people, wildlife."

"Yeah?"

"It is."

"That could be attractive. It's an island, right?"

"Off South Africa, I think. Definitely in that area."

Howard winced as he put weight on the injured leg. It made Will think of him for the first time as brittle. Something like a shadow passed over his face, then he said, "Of course, there is another option. You and I could take off and tell the cops the whole thing." He held up his car keys and tinkled them. "We'll tell them Jake killed the cop, show them that film. We'll say he forced us to help him hide the body, threatening us with the crossbow. What do you say? We need to get a story straight, and I think we can scrape through it. Don't answer me right now. Don't say anything. Think about it. Just think. That's all. It's not like you owe him anything." They stepped out of the water and stood on pebbles. "Have you seen the crossbow? I thought I left it there."

A rustling, and Jake stepped out from the treeline. "I've got it."

Will felt that Howard and he were a couple of naughty kids who had to justify themselves. He didn't want to revisit what had happened; he hoped they could all turn their backs on the whole episode and never mention it again. He said, "You came down," just to say something, knowing it was inane. "How are you feeling?"

"She escaped."

"Yeah," said Howard. "She's in there somewhere." He pointed beyond the lake at the dense mass of green. "Hey, that thing's loaded. Be careful: we don't want another accident."

"What's happening now?" said Jake.

Howard shrugged. "Plan B, I guess." Water dripped off him, leaving dark circles on stones.

"There is no plan B," said Jake, and shot him. Howard staggered and flapped his arms, a crossbow bolt protruding from his neck. He fell on his knees, and Will caught his concerned gaze. A jet of blood spurted, and a grotesque gargling sound came from Howard's throat. His knees trembled, then failed, and he fell into shallow water.

35

Will stood perfectly still, with the idea that, if he moved, a similar thing would happen to him. Howard lay face down in shallow water with a dark stain spreading around his head. His bandana had slipped off and, as Will watched, it was picked up by the current and borne away.

Will could hardly believe this. There was something dreamlike about it. All the violence was coming at him so casually, happening before he knew it. He couldn't get set for it. Again he had been caught off balance and not concentrating. And now it was too late, there was nothing to be done but think about what he should have done.

"Jake?" For the moment he had no thought for his own safety, only a sense of outrage and confusion. "What did you do that for?"

"I know what plan B is. I saw you cooking it up. Plan B was Howard and Will going to the cops, fessing up and letting Jake hang. I couldn't let that happen."

"But—"

Jake nodded at the green. "It's worked out," he said lightly. "We say that we were attacked by bandits. Probably happens all the time. Bandits from over the border, half-naked guys with red teeth. They tried to rob us.

There was a fight. They killed Howard and the girl, and we escaped. And – this is pretty clever, you have to admit it – they killed the cop, too. We could even say we saw them do it. See? It squares the whole thing."

"The girl's gone."

"That girl's not going anywhere. I've been in there. There's no way out. Cliffs on either side, and the river goes over some mean rapids. We'll find her easily. There's nowhere for her to go."

"I'm not—"

"It's that. That's what it is. You and me together. It's you and me together now, mate."

"Jake, come on."

Howard's body turned slowly in an eddy at the side of a boulder, accompanied by pretty swoops and whirls of pink water. Jake prised the Jeep keys from his hand. The little toy robot swung. It seemed a strange thing for a middle-aged man to carry – have carried, rather. Will hoped it didn't mean he had a child somewhere. Considering that made him sad, sadder than the body did. Like everything else Howard owned, it was now orphaned.

"Jake, I think you need to stop and think, and realise that you are having a very bad comedown, and the way you are thinking is really twisted. I want you to snap out . . . Please . . ."

He realised Jake was reloading the crossbow, drawing into himself, seeming to become smaller and more concentrated, tightening himself as well as the bowstring.

"Jake, come on. Come on."

Jake did not answer or look him in the eye. Will considered the cold geometry laid out before him. Dead Howard was no longer a factor, he was just part of the scenery. There was only Jake, the path and the pool. Jake was over a dozen paces away. Maybe Will could get to the man before he finished reloading, but probably not. If he tried to swim across the pool, Jake would have a shot before he got to the other side. The path was closest. There were boulders to hide behind. And it led upwards, into light, out of this shadow zone. He sprinted for it.

Jake shouted after him. "Where are you going? Where are you going? Will, don't be ridiculous. I'm not going to shoot you, you idiot." It was annoying that Jake's voice sounded as reasonable as ever.

Will scrambled over rock, then hauled himself up a root to cut out a switchback. Convinced that Jake had the crossbow raised and aimed, he could feel its gaze scouring the rock, hunting him out, and he was acutely aware of every vertebra and the soft places on either side.

Jake was shouting, "You want her to die, don't you? You know as well as I do the situation we're in. You're not objecting." Will hardly heard; he was just glad Jake was shouting. It seemed to make it less likely that the man would shoot. "Look at you. Staying out of everything. You pretend you're not involved and it's nothing to do with you. Come back. Where are you going to go? What are you going to do?"

Stopping was bad. At least running away was actively accomplishing something. Now he had gone and given Jake time to zero in on his exit. The next area of decent cover was at least five paces away, and the path to it was narrow and the incline steady. He would make a tempting target.

"I'm not going to shoot you – what do you think I am? All right, look, I'm putting the crossbow down. See? Can you see, Will?"

The girl had run a similar gauntlet. If she could summon the strength to do it, so could he. This rock was in the shade, and its surface was cold. Will wanted to hug it, lie all night beside it. Acting was not so difficult, but waiting and feeling the fear crowding in were hard. He wished fervently, harder than he had ever wished for anything, to not be here. Anywhere else would do.

He shouted, "This is fucking nuts." The situation had come so quickly and out of nowhere that it was hard to believe. There was an element of playacting about his actions. Jake's, too, he suspected. The unfamiliar roles were not yet fully inhabited.

Will could not imagine running up the path, but he could picture the route to the next area of cover. He encouraged himself with the thought that every step he took made any shot harder. He grabbed a rock and hauled it over his shoulder. He hoped Jake would look at it tumbling down and spoil the bead he had drawn.

Before he had even completed the thought, as if surprising himself would surprise Jake, too, Will dived out of his hiding place and scrambled upwards, feeling his exposure like a tingle across his skin. It took an effort not to turn around and return to hiding. He gulped the last bit of space, threw himself down hard and fell badly, banging his knee. He snatched hold of a root and pressed himself into the dirt. Thorns pressed into his back.

He was aware of Jake shouting, and peeked. "Will, I'm not going to shoot you. He had lain the crossbow down and was sitting on a rock some half a dozen metres from it, shading his eyes as he looked up. "See? You're my fucking mate. Come back. Or don't. Stay up there if you want. Come down, don't come down, it makes no difference to me."

Will plunged on, turning, running, grabbing at rocks and roots. A growl came from between his gritted teeth. Every lash and sting felt welcome, it was more stuff between him and the mess below. He swivelled and turned (these switchbacks were so cruel), ran, fell, scrambled, jumped – and suddenly he was on sunny level ground.

He lay and panted, tickled by grass, feeling the thrill of simple existence, the joy of security. He looked up at the unanswering sky, happy to inhabit his body. No one was shooting at him, and that was enough to spread dumb contentment. Perhaps he could close his eyes and magic would happen; he would drift off and awake elsewhere. He fantasised, too, about a shower and a drink.

Of course Jake wasn't coming for him, and had no intention of killing him. He was irrelevant – it was the girl who mattered. With the witness disposed of, there was no one for Will to save except himself, no reason to do anything but get with the plan.

Will's camera sat on the grass by the Jeep. It seemed fine; it had got a little dirty, but there was nothing wrong with the lens.

It would be very good to sit here and rest. Presently, Jake would join him. He would no longer be carrying the crossbow, though perhaps there would be blood on him. Will would know without asking. They would eye each other up silently, then drive away. They would have to talk eventually, to get the story straight – how many bandits, where they came from, the nature of the attack. After some hours, they would get to a village and try to get the story across through mime and diagrams. Their wounds would be dressed, and there would be much concern. Eventually policemen would arrive, and they would be questioned. They would be taken back here, and made to show where events happened, and perhaps would watch the remains of the policeman being recovered from the pool.

Guiltily, Will wondered whether he wanted all this to happen. After all, it was a solution. Maybe he did want what he could not allow himself to think he wanted. The efforts to help the girl were tokens to salve his conscience. He was a coward and a hypocrite because he couldn't face an ugliness he secretly knew was necessary. Jake, at least, was honest about getting his hands dirty, not afraid to take on the burden of an onerous and unpleasant necessity. Will was contemptible for trying halfheartedly to dodge it, doing just enough to tell himself he wasn't involved, to sidestep guilt.

He got up. There was no choice, then; he knew what he had to do. His heart heavy, he started jogging, puffing heavily, away from the Jeep, down the track.

In no immediate danger, with the spiky sharpness of adrenalin fading, he realised how much pain he was in, and as a kind of academic exercise, merely to keep other thoughts at bay, he tried once again to trace the source of each injury. That tenderness on the side of his head – oh, yes, he had hit it against the side of the Jeep in simpler times, when his only problem had been a runaway Jeep.

What a lark that now seemed, an amusing little farce. The stinging lacerations on his arms must have come from twigs and thorns. His left palm had been cut by the girl's blade, but when had he skinned his right? It seemed cruel that, on top of everything, he had picked up a sprinkling of itchy bites.

When he came to a fallen tree he recognised, he stopped and stood with his hands on his knees, gasping for breath. As hoped, the youth and his grandfather squatted there, in a glade just off the path, pretty much exactly where he had left them.

36

Will smiled and waved. The two men looked balefully back. They seemed irritable and bleary. Their earlier high spirits had diminished, and they had sunk into a drunken dullness.

As he approached, they blinked and made an effort to focus their eyes. Will supposed he must be a startling sight, filthy and wounded. But they did not exhibit much curiosity. He could hardly be their favourite person.

"So," Will said stupidly, between gasps for breath. He was aware of no longer being a novelty item, this pale dirty guy who kept appearing and mugging dumbly away, the player of a cruel and unnecessary trick. "I'm sorry, all right. Sorry I threw your bottle away. That was bad of me. He pointed at the crossbow. "I want to buy that."

He took all his money out of his wallet. A couple of the red hundreds, a few blue notes, some brown ones – surely it was enough. After all, Jake had bought his with a couple of bottles of booze.

The old man took the wallet. His hands were darker than the rest of him and heavily lined, with gnarly knuckles. The smooth and skinny arms seemed almost youthful in contrast. "You want the wallet, too? Sure, take it. It's good leather."

The old man took out the cards and started examining them. He was particularly taken by the hologram on Will's bank card, turning it in to make it flicker in the light and discussing it with the youth. They had the lumbering, careful look of very drunk people trying to appear sober.

"Have that, too. Why not?"

The old man put it back in the wallet, along with the library card and the Tesco Clubcard, careful to get them back in what he thought was the right order. In doing so, he discovered Will's photo of Jess. He took it out and pointed at it, then at Will.

"Yes," Will said, "that's my girlfriend. Well – was."

The old man held the photo at arm's length, slightly raised, and put a hand on his heart. Then he pointed at the crossbow and nodded. He said something to the kid and laughed. Will asked, "What? What? You want to keep the photo? You'll give me your crossbow in exchange for the photo? Is that it?"

The old man wagged a finger. He looked up dreamily and pressed the photo against the embarrassed lips of the youth, who batted it away.

"You want the girl?" Will grinned. "As a wife for him, right?" Here they were, men together, sharing a bawdy joke, the kid growing up, being shown the ways of his elders. Will smiled wanly, but perhaps the old man sensed his unease, because he put the photo in the wallet and gave it back. Both men were talking and waving, and Will had the sense that they were apologising – it was only a joke, don't take offence.

Will wished he had some more booze to give them. He told himself to be patient. The worst thing with drunks was to get annoyed. Then he would never get what he wanted.

The youth pointed at his camera, and Will turned it on. He showed the pictures that he had taken earlier of the three of them grinning together. There was Will, the lost tourist, with the guys on either side. The kid gestured at the camera, then at the crossbow, and finally, Will realised his meaning.

"I get it. You want the picture? But I can't print it out for you. Not like that one."

They settled into their positions. Will felt dismissed; it was as if he weren't even there. He put himself back into the old man's eyeline and smiled weakly.

"Please, I just want your crossbow. Just . . . I need this, the crossbow. Please. I can't give you the girl, but you can have all the money in the wallet, and the wallet itself, and any of the stuff in there that you find interesting, like the card or the photo or whatever. For the crossbow. Come on. It's . . . about five hundred yuan. That's a lot of money right there. The wallet itself is worth, well, it's worth a few hundred, I guess."

The youth grinned and tapped the camera.

"You want to swap the camera for the crossbow? No way, this is a serious piece of equipment – come on. Look, I'll give you . . ." He stopped. Anything he said would be obscene. He was quibbling while a girl was being hunted. "Sure, have it."

So Will swapped his Canon SLR for a homemade crossbow, a pouch of four quarrels and a jar of beeswax. He watched the exchange as if it were someone else's hands doing it. What a pain this girl was proving to be, this girl he owed nothing to, whom he didn't even like, whose name he had forgotten.

Will showed the kid how to flick between pictures. He held the camera by the lens and pressed the buttons on the back. Well, it was his now; he could touch it where he wanted. In a couple of hours, the battery would run down and the picture show would be over. Then the cumbersome thing would be thrown in the bush, or maybe the old guy would take it to a village and swap it, or perhaps the youth would get himself to a town and sell it.

As a fool easily parted from his wealth, Will knew he had lost their respect, and it was awkward to be there. He turned and began a stumbling, exhausted jog back down the track.

At the clifftop, nothing had changed in his absence. It was still a beautiful spot. It would be lovely to be coming on it for the first time. The crossbow seemed makeshift and ordinary, a primitive piece of farm equipment. He supposed he must at least practise with it. Setting the butt against his belly, with the end of the stock against the ground, he pulled the bowstring back. It was like working an exercise machine set for too much resistance, and his face reddened with the effort. By the time the trigger clicked into position and locked, his arms were shaking. His stomach was sore where the butt had rested, and pressure lines were drawn across his tingling, red fingers where the string had dug in. The wood creaked, then seemed to settle. He could feel the stored power; it seemed alert and humming.

The quarrels were shorter and thicker than bow arrows. He rolled them in a palm and squinted down them. They were skilfully made, straight and true, almost perfectly cylindrical. Only up close could he see the marks and abrasions that showed they had been laboriously whittled and sanded rather than stamped out in a factory. The delicate fletching was not plastic, as he had assumed, but some thin wood – he guessed bamboo – pounded flat, folded and cut.

He smeared beeswax along a quarrel and laid it in the groove. Its back didn't quite reach the string, as he'd expected it to, and he wondered if these were defectively short. But there was no rear notch, as there would be with an arrow. Perhaps the fact that the string was already moving when it met the quarrel helped propel it with more force.

He hefted it on his shoulder. It was heavy and awkward and hard to steady. At least it was simple to aim; you sighted along the quarrel. But that meant dipping his head right down, more than you would with a gun, so that his cheek was almost horizontal. He groped his hand along the stock, looking for the bone trigger, which made the thing waver and shake. When he did find it, he reckoned he was lucky not to shoot his own foot. He started again, this time getting down on one knee to steady himself.

Aiming at a tree trunk, Will settled, held his breath, depressed the trigger and tensed for something to happen. As he was wondering whether he'd been sold a dud, the trigger clicked and gave in, the machine jolted, and the quarrel vanished quietly, with no snap or kick, catapulted tremendously fast into the green. Now he had only three

shots left. Still, the exercise had been worthwhile: he had
learned that the trigger was stiff, and that if he wanted to
get off an accurate shot he'd have to get the thing aimed
quickly, as he couldn't hold it steady for longer than a few
seconds.

Will looked over the cliff edge. Cliffs frowned down
almost sheer on either side of the river. After a couple of
hundred metres, the ravine narrowed and the cliffs were
lower, but here the forest was choking. There was no way
out. For the girl, it was a wedge-shaped prison. She was
down in there somewhere, in those hunting grounds,
trapped with a few hundred square metres to hide in. Jake
was in there too, prowling. Or Will could be too late; the
thing could be over.

Will took a long look at the Jeep. Everything about it
was sturdily reassuring; even the tyres looked pretty.
Sluggishness stole over him, and as his resolve wavered
the end of the crossbow dipped. There was no guarantee
that Jake would get anywhere with his hunt. Besides, it
was hot, and he was tired. He turned away and stepped
onto the path. He knew it well enough now to place his
feet without looking. Feeling pompous and a little daft,
and not at all deadly, he held the crossbow awkwardly
upright like a standard. He tried to think about putting
down one foot after another and hoped he wasn't making
much noise. It occurred to him that if Jake were anywhere
around the pool, Will would make an easy target. Still, at
least this time he could shoot back.

He stopped beside a large flat boulder – an old friend
– and considered the river where it flowed away from
the pool. The river seemed playful as it split at the rocks,

frothing and jostling, forming translucent bell shapes where it flowed over smooth stones, doodling spirals and corkscrews. Then the various streams came together, and the narrowing channel gave a sense of seriousness and purpose as it fell down a succession of steep steps.

On either side, the forest was thick but not impossible to move through – the grass was about waist-high. Will saw a blue flash, just a flicker out of the corner of his eye, but he convinced himself that it had to be Jake, that he had glimpsed denim shorts. He could think of nothing natural that might be that colour. Jake was about fifty metres into the ravine, on this side of the river, which was pretty much where Will had expected him to be.

Will's heart was beating wildly, and he realised with annoyance that he was shaking. He was in no state to steady and fire a crossbow, and this scene had hardly begun. He tried to tell himself to calm down, but that didn't work, so he thought about how absurd the situation was, really, when you considered it. To think that he was crouching here holding a crossbow and seriously considering aiming it at Jake. He shook his head in dumb disbelief, and that wry acknowledgement seemed to do it.

Will went down to the beach and headed away from the falls into the trees, looking all around except at Howard's body. He swished through the dense waist-high grass. The buzz of insects and the gurgle of water helped cover the sound of leaves crackling and twigs breaking. He tried to keep the crossbow level before him, but that made it hard to move stealthily. A leafy branch knocked the quarrel from its notch, and he had to stop and grope to find it.

He saw Jake about ten metres ahead, moving along in a crouch. The crossbow was braced with the butt against his stomach, so it pointed where he looked. Sadly, he did not appear at all like a cold, calculating killer; he looked like a mate.

Jake saw Will and rose. "You've come to help. That's great."

"I've come to stop you."

"Stop pointing that thing at me, someone will get hurt."

"Put yours down. Put it down."

Jake snorted. "Don't be ridiculous. Look at you, you're absurd. You're actually aiming at me, at your friend, who is in the habit of doing you good turns and is doing you one now. Go back to the Jeep and I'll see you up there in a bit." There was no madness in his voice, and his words all sounded reasonable. Will hardly heard them; his focus was on the crossbow Jake held at the level of his chest. It was levelling and arcing round – just by slow degrees, but there was undeniably an intention there.

Will shouted, "Drop it." His voice was an unfamiliar hoarse bark, but he was pleased to hear some strength in it. He was not faltering yet.

"Or what? You'll shoot me? You don't think that's a bit of a daft idea? You maybe want to think it through a bit. I'm going to have to do this. I'm going to have to aim at you now. Look what you made me do. There."

Jake took a last little step and settled his shoulders down into the crossbow, his upper body bending and tightening. Will could not see anything of the quarrel except the sharpened tip. That meant it was aimed right at his head. Behind it, a narrowed eye burned.

Will wanted badly to leap aside. A butterfly with brilliant blue wings wavered ahead, a flickering visitation that seemed to have no relation to the rest of the scene. An unbidden mental image came of the butterfly pinned against a board. Will could be skewered just as easily.

"If you shoot me," said Will, "I'll shoot you."

"Yeah, same."

Will turned sideways, keeping the crossbow aimed at Jake but making himself a smaller target. He was acutely conscious of how much defenceless flesh he was made of. His skin tingled. They were about fifteen paces apart. Swarms of tiny insects gave the illusion that the air between them was alive with swirling currents. Will's arms were beginning to hurt with the effort of keeping his weapon steady, and he knew it would waver soon. How disappointing if that was all it came down to – a test of strength.

Jake talked on, sounding exasperated. "Look at us. Will you look at this. What a fucking mess. Put it down, and go away. I'll be with you in a bit." It was annoying that he sounded so normal.

Will answered slowly, rebuilding his purpose in his mind. "Leave the girl alone."

"What do you think is going to happen? You save her and get married? She doesn't give a fuck. She's going to get you killed. She's going to tell people what she saw and we are going to get executed." He repeated the word, drawing it out, as if it was the summary of his argument, and the word could sway by its dreaded tone. "Executed."

37

The crossbow, Will realised, was not really like a gun, though it was fired the same way. A gun surely could not have this sense of vitality and energy. The thing creaked irritably, and somehow the tightness of the drawn string was being communicated to his arms through the stock. Sighting, he could see scratches and abrasions all the way down the quarrel, which brought its maker to mind. Jake had already shot two people with his, and that, he felt, gave him a considerable advantage. He knew the trick of it, how to join the machine to his will, to think or cheat yourself into pulling the trigger. Maybe the man was building up to it now, and firing would happen, in due and proper course, as the conclusion of a long thought process: or perhaps the way to do it was not think about it at all, let the finger twitch like an involuntary tic, so that it came as a surprise.

Will said, "She's never going to talk, she's too frightened. Let's go up to the Jeep and just . . . leave. I won't even tell anyone what you did to Howard. We'll say he vanished."

"Well, that's big of you. I appreciate your efforts. But it's not going to work." Jake sighed, and said, "Okay, whatever," and twisted quickly and sank out of sight. He was gone so thoroughly that he could have blinked out of existence. Only a branch twanging back and forth indicated that he had ever been there.

Will ducked, and his heart started pounding wildly. Now what? What had Jake meant? But there was no point in picking over the exchange. All that had happened, really, was that he had given away the only advantage he had – that of surprise. A sense of satisfaction at having not shirked from aiming or being aimed at leaked away.

Down here in the bristling grass, he could barely see a metre ahead. If Jake came crawling towards him, they might not notice each other till their noses bumped. It was unnerving to be so unsighted, and he felt a strong urge to rise. Just as strong was the desire to slink back to the Jeep, having done all he could. Both moves, he told himself, would be equally dumb. He stayed right where he was, trembling and needing a drink.

"This is black and white," shouted Jake. "You're with me or against me."

"You know what I'll say."

"I want to hear it."

"I'm against you."

Jake had retreated, but it was hard to judge how far. "You'd better go away. Go back to the Jeep. If I see you down here, I'll shoot you. Is that clear? And for what? For nothing. I won't shoot you if you go up there, on the cliff."

Will was listening so hard, the skin of his cheeks was tightening. He realised that Jake was moving after each statement. That seemed prudent, and Will followed suit, duckwalking sideways for a couple of paces. But the ground dipped sharply, and leaves the size of his palm, damp and thick, closed around him till he was in them up to his neck. Impossible, in this position, to bring the crossbow to bear, and he was making a lot of noise.

His secret hope, which kept nagging at him, was that he could just stay here and not be seen. His courage left him, and all he wanted was his life. He stopped. Everything was shaking. He looked down and saw his hands holding the crossbow, how they had shaped to it and warmed it, and this steadied him, and he began to believe in this little drama. He worried that he had lost his spare quarrels, and took his hand off the crossbow to feel them, extending from his thigh pocket. He set them to the side, so that the flat edges were poking his stomach and he would know they were there without looking.

He came out and headed forward. He was aware of a set of unhelpful reactions to his situation that were stored behind a mental dam, but he did not want to consider that, as even to think about the dam would weaken it. What a lot of mental tricks there were to this business. It was all in the head. Just to stay in this, just to continue moving and breathing and watching, seemed to require all his energy. It helped to give himself clear mental orders – 'Put this foot here, move these thorns, duck here' – and he was even moving his dry, cracked lips. 'Sweep left, sweep right, step here. Don't let the crossbow fall, don't get caught up in the branches, come on now, keep steady, stay low.'

What was Jake doing? Would he be systematic, quartering the ground, or patrolling, going round and round in a circle? Of course, it was quite possible that they would not see each other again, or the girl either, and would keep creeping past each other till nightfall. Darkness would not solve anything, though; Jake would just go and cover the path up to the clifftop to stop any attempt at escape.

Will came to an area of slightly higher ground, thick with grass and ferns. He was in the shadow of the frowning cliffs. The persistent rustle of rapids was loud here. The water sounded fast and rough. The ground banked steeply down towards it. He was deep in the gorge and heading towards its narrowest point, where the parallel cliffs, shaggy with greenery, almost came together. He had arrived at the limits of these hunting grounds – it was impossible to go farther into the steeply rising, deeply forested land. He thought about turning and starting a trek back into the sunshine, but he told himself that he hadn't yet gone through all the correct motions. If the girl was killed, he wanted to say that he did more than buy a crossbow and tramp through the woods and make threats. There was still much to be done before it could be settled that he had tried his best.

He sensed a change in the pattern of sound around him – a new modulation to the insect hum, and he relaxed and let his attention find a thread and follow it, and that took his head, for the first time, upwards, and he saw the girl. She was buried deep in a tree, brown limbs wrapped tightly around a trunk, looking like she wanted to be swallowed into it. Her soles were pressed against the bark and her toes dug in as hard as fingers. It seemed an odd choice, to hide up there when the grass was so long. Perhaps it was built into her, a cultural thing: this was how you hid from predators.

"Hey!" He pointed the weapon away and waved her down. "Come on," he hissed. "Let's go. Come on, if I wanted to shoot you I'd have done it already, wouldn't I?"

She pointed, then the finger waggled with urgency. Will turned, saw bushes rustle, then the outline of a head and a body took shape out of the green. A moment later, Jake was right there. He had not seen the girl; all his attention was directed at Will. He was sweating a great deal: the mud on his face was streaked where droplets had run down it. He fell to one knee and raised his crossbow. Will dived heedlessly sideways, and something bit his arm. As he hit the ground, it seemed to strike again; it was as if some animal was attacking him. Blood trickled down his wrist and plopped onto a leaf. He grimaced. Jake had shot him; the quarrel had scraped a raw red slash above his elbow. Will gritted his teeth against the sting and told himself that he was lucky, that this pain was just a little warning. If he didn't sharpen up, there would be more, and worse.

Will's hand found his crossbow and just the feel of the wood told him that the bowstring was still drawn. Something like pleasure came – and the pain was forgotten – when he realised where they stood; he had a readied weapon and Jake's was slack. The hurt in his arm was a spur. He stood, shouldered the crossbow, and ran forward. Jake turned and ran away.

Will had the idea that the crossbow, held before him, could plough through the green like the bow of a ship through water, but in practice it just snagged branches, and wiry tendrils tugged it aside. He saw the wisdom of running with it the way the tribal men did, with the thing unloaded and slung over one shoulder, so he did that, holding the quarrel in his other hand. Up ahead, Jake tripped and fell and scrambled furiously out of a bush, and Will knew that this was his moment. Quite calmly, he got the quarrel into the groove and got the crossbow up and against his shoulder. In less than a second, with a beautiful harmonious motion, he had built the shot. Jake was right there, blundering up a rise, thrashing at twigs and leaves as if they were a net that trapped him. His T-shirt stuck to his back, and Will could see the bumps of his spine. It was a big target, and there was plenty of time.

The weapon seemed to whisper – to be fired was what it wanted – and Will's finger felt for the cool bone curl of the trigger, as thoughtless and natural a gesture as putting an arm through a sleeve. He felt an abstract curiosity, both to see if he could hit his target and to find out what this thing could do to a human. Just a twitch of the finger, it could happen casually and almost without intention.

Then Jake looked back, and Will saw the fear on his face, and his shot disintegrated. He relaxed his arms and watched Jake scramble noisily away. Had he really nearly done that? It was as if a delirium had come over him, a full recovery had been made in moments, and the passing of that feeling left nothing behind. Who was he to be here thinking that?

He tramped back to the girl, now crouched at the base of the tree. She stank of blood and dirt. Her body seemed smaller than he remembered, her limbs thinner, eyes wider and whiter. She had lost her bright red headband, or thrown it away perhaps for being too noticeable, and now bedraggled hair swept across her face. Her skirt was bunched between her legs and tucked or tied up in some way.

All they had to do was get back to the falls and up the path. He led the girl down to the river and along the bank till he found a crossing point. "We go over here, then along on the other side. See? He won't expect it." He didn't know if she understood, but she saw the wisdom of the move. When he waded in, she followed. Will knew they were dangerously exposed while they crossed, and he stepped in a kind of shuffling backwards dance, keeping the cross-bow levelled, barely aware of the water frothing round his thighs. It was easier with her there; it made his purpose concrete. He was hard and certain, closed in. He would get this girl out, and if he saw Jake he would shoot him. "No need to worry," he told her, almost jauntily. "He's in there, running around. Doesn't have a clue."

On this side of the river the bushes were denser and the ground rose steeply upwards. They splashed along at the edge of the water, ducking overhanging branches. Every step was a problem: how to stay upright and in cover, and keep the crossbow in play. It was good that they were making rapid progress, but he wasn't sure if this was smart. Well, if it worked, it was. They followed a bend and the clifftop came into view. He leaped forward in his mind to being up there, and when he wrenched himself back he grew anxious. The trick was not to be anywhere but here, really present. It was cold here in the water and the rocks were slippery, but it was better than being in the dark forest. There were fewer insects, and the oppressive mugginess that had been over him like a blanket was lifted. There was a clean and clear feeling to the air. It was good that he could see so much sky, and more with every step.

They came to the last set of rapids. The water here seemed playful as it spit at the rocks, frothing and jostling, forming translucent bell shapes where it flowed over smooth stones, doodling spirals and corkscrews. He clambered onto a rock and lay down. It was all there out before him. He could see up ahead the pale rocks and the channels of water, and beyond, the pool and the falls, and then, out at the limit of the scene, the top of the cliff where it was safe.

The girl came up and put a hand on his shoulder to steady herself, or perhaps to remind him that she was there. She was frowning as she scanned the scene. Her fingers dug into him, pushing him down, then she was past him, running. Her feet splashed, high-stepping out of the water onto a white rock. She hopped to a larger boulder, ran along that, then got down and waded upstream along a channel. She had seen the path up the cliff and it was too much for her – she was greedy for it. Her tied-up skirt unfurled and she held it bunched up with one hand.

Will worried that his earlier assumption was wrong, that Jake was not thrashing through the forest at all, but was here and very close. He knew how Jake played his first-person shooters: he was notorious for hiding with a sniper rifle at a high vantage point, picking off infuriated enemies who never worked out where they'd been hit from. If he had the wits to apply similar tactics to this, he would be here, on the beach or by the lake, where the sight lines and the cover were good.

Will laid the crossbow down on the boulder and considered the terrain, looking at the scene against the current: flowing river to still lake to falls, bush to beach to path.

The retreating girl was to his right and would soon be at the beach. His ears picked up the clue. Above the roar of the falls, he heard splashing. Jake was to his left, coming along the far side of the pool, over the little stones. He was moving faster than her, and no doubt he was trying to get a little closer before taking a shot.

Will took the crossbow and thought of it as a puzzle. He had to be clever about how he was going to do it. If he just popped up, Jake might see him, and it would be down to chance. He rose slowly and knelt with one foot flat on the rock and one knee in a crevice.

Jake stopped and crouched down. He was only ten paces away from her, and she hadn't even seen him. He hunched down into his machine. Will brought his cross-bow up. He wasn't going to warn Jake, not this time, and he wasn't going to let anything break the shot.

38

As Will sighted down the bolt, his vision narrowed to a tunnel. The things in the tunnel were sharp and beautifully detailed, and all around was a smear. Will felt a strange intimacy with Jake: they were joined together, he had made a frame to consider him in, and he had rarely looked so intensely at another human. An enormous indifference came over him, an indifference that took in not only Jake and the girl, but himself. A kind of singing hum entered him, and the river and the cliff and the trees held their breath. He fired, and Jake cried out and fell into the water.

Will rose and pulled back the bowstring. He was at home doing it now; the string clicked neatly into place like a puzzle piece. He loaded it unhurriedly then climbed carefully down off the rock into the shallows.

The girl had turned and was standing, holding her skirt around her waist. She looked with fierce concentration at Jake, who was on his knees, water up to his ribs. He was holding shattered wood. Will's shot had been true: the quarrel had slammed into the stock of his crossbow and ruined it. Jake dropped the remains, and they were snatched by the current and spun away. His arms and hands were flecked with blood. "You shot me."

"I shot your crossbow. You got hit by splinters."

"You could have killed me."

"I guess. Yeah. But I didn't." Will settled the crossbow into his shoulder, breathing easily.

"You going to shoot me again?"

"I'm thinking about it."

The girl splashed towards them. "You played this very well. She's your little dog now, isn't she? You're her fucking hero."

"Give me the Jeep keys."

"Here."

He threw them, and Will plucked them from shallow water. "Let's go. Let's go up the path. Come on. You first. I've got this trained on you. Next time, I'll aim for your spine."

"Well done. Now we're both going to get killed."

Will turned for a last look at the place. It was pretty. He was aware that Howard's body was not too far away in the shallows but, as he couldn't see it, it didn't bother him. The sun was starting to set and the light was soft and diffuse, the shadows mellow. A good time to take a picture.

Jake scooted bad-temperedly up the hill, and Will kept a steady five or six paces back. The girl followed far behind. She was still wary, and clearly didn't want to be anywhere near Jake.

When they got to the top, Jake crouched and said, "I'm really tired."

"Been a long day."

"So. What are we going to do?"

"I'm going to the police. With the girl. I'm going to tell them everything. Down to the smallest detail."

"Well done. We'll both be executed. I hope you're happy."

"I think I'll be okay. I've got this." Will tucked the crossbow against his chest to free one hand, and took out Howard's keyring. He popped open the top of the little robot's head and showed Jake the SD card. "The film from the camera. That's got your admission of guilt on it. And, of course, the girl will testify to everything she saw – you shooting Howard, me trying to save her."

"That's slender. They'll still blame you. You were trying to cover up a murder."

"I think I can prove duress. Anyway, I'll take my chances."

"They'll shoot me, though."

"Yeah, I guess. Bullet in the back of the head. If they catch you."

Will threw the keys at his feet.

"I said I was going to go to the police. I didn't say when. I'll tell them everything, but I'll change this bit. I'll say you attacked me, got the Jeep keys and drove off. Going to be quite a while before the alarm gets raised. Me and the lady got to get to her village, then I don't suppose there's a phone signal for miles – no, you'll have hours. Maybe days, even. I'll delay the thing as long as I can."

Jake picked up the keys.

"Head straight for Laos. Get as close to the border as you can, then dump the Jeep and go in through the forest at night. Play it right and you'll be deep in before the hunt starts. Of course, it'll be sketchy. You'll have to steal money, a passport. But I'm sure you'll work it out."

"I'll have to live my whole life on the run. I'll never be safe. Thanks for nothing."

"Here she comes. Go on, get out of here. There are worse things. There's a lot of places to hide. I hear Madagascar's nice."

Jake opened the door to the Jeep. "Least I tried." He pulled himself up to his full height, then got slowly in. But his attempt at a dignified entry was sabotaged, absurdly: an angry blob, or something like it, rocketed through his legs and in surprise he fell on his backside. Will glimpsed the scales on the pangolin's back, then it was gone, just a receding rustle, and Jake was bundling himself into the Jeep. Of course, the thing had been skulking under the driver's seat.

The engine wouldn't catch, and Will felt awkward: this was a stuttering, fluffed exit. When it did start, on the fifth time, it juddered away with a panicky roar. It was gone almost as quickly as the pangolin.

"Happy running," Will called, though he doubted Jake heard him.

Will's camera was hanging from a tree. At first, in the fading light, he thought it was a bat. It was muddy but intact, though the battery was drained. The boy must have put it there for him to find. Perhaps, when the screen had died, the novelty had faded, or maybe the old man and his grandson had regretted the unfair trade and wished to return it. Perhaps it had seemed too cumbersome to carry home, and they had worried someone would think they'd stolen it. There were many possible motives, and no one to ask.

He could hear the girl coming, so he fired the crossbow into the trees and dropped it. He arranged himself on the ground and rubbed his jaw as if he'd been hit and was coming out of a daze. The girl arrived, puffing from the climb, and when she saw his condition, her eyes widened in alarm.

"It's fine. But he hit me and stole the Jeep." They listened for a while to the whine of the retreating engine. When it could no longer be heard, she began to examine his wounds, talking and tutting to him softly. Howard's word 'consensual' came to him. He closed his eyes and it felt pleasant, despite everything, to be in this moment. From nowhere, he remembered her name, and said it aloud – "Qiong Mei." She kept on cooing and talking, and the noise was calming, reminding him a little of running water, so he closed his eyes to hear it better.